Scribners

MIDWINTER
MYSTERIES
1

MIDWINTER MYSTERIES
1

Edited by
HILARY HALE

Maurice Maguire

Christmas 1991

from Mammy & Daddy

Scribners

A Scribners Book

First published in Great Britain in 1991 by Scribners
a Division of Macdonald & Co (Publishers) Ltd
London & Sydney

Collection copyright © Macdonald & Co 1991

The stories are copyright respectively:
© Robert Barnard 1991
© Simon Brett 1991
© Michael Gilbert 1991
© H.R.F. Keating 1991
© Roger Longrigg 1991
© Peter Lovesey Limited 1991
© John Malcolm 1991
© M.D. Ripley 1991
© Margaret Yorke 1991

British Library Cataloguing in Publication Data

Midwinter mysteries: 1.
I. Hale, Hilary
823[F]

ISBN 0–356–19781–6

Photoset in North Wales by
Derek Doyle & Associates, Mold, Clwyd.
Printed and bound in Great Britain by
Mackays of Chatham PLC, Chatham, Kent

Scribners
A Division of
Macdonald & Co (Publishers) Ltd
165 Great Dover Street
London SE1 4YA
A member of Maxwell Macmillan Publishing Corporation

Contents

Contents

Editor's Note

The short story has played an integral role in the development and popularity of mystery fiction. Since the heyday of *Scribner's* and *Strand* magazines the outlets for murder and mayhem in small bites have sadly diminished, although the publication of various anthologies and collections has to some extent fulfilled the demand from a loyal and discerning readership.

So it is a great pleasure to create a new volume with *Midwinter Mysteries* and to bring Scribners and the crime short story together again.

The principle of the collection is to provide varied, puzzling and satisfying mysteries – a tenet which has been met with subtlety and enthusiasm by the distinguished contributors. I would like to thank them all for the quality and ingenuity of their stories and for the pleasure they have given me in bringing them together.

Hilary Hale

MIDWINTER
MYSTERIES
1

The Stuff of Nightmares

Robert Barnard

The Stuff of Nightmares

STRANGELY ENOUGH I'D THOUGHT OF Wicklow only the week before. I'd been reading a review in the *Times Literary Supplement* of a life of Hemingway, and reacted to the assertion: 'All bullies are something else underneath, of course.' I'd shaken my head. Wicklow wasn't, I said to myself; Wicklow was just bully through and through.

And now here he was on the other side of a smoky Glasgow bar – the body even heavier, the face jowlier, the hair flecked with grey, but still unmistakably the Wicklow of my schooldays thirty-five years on. I shivered uncontrollably and buried my head in the *Literary Review*.

Perhaps it was not so strange that I'd thought of Wicklow so recently: I think he comes to my mind whenever instances of legalised cruelty come up – and heaven knows, that's often enough these days. It must have been 1960 when I saw him last, but that was two or three years after he had left Manorfield School. He used periodically to revisit the scene of his triumphs. The period of his greatest dominance was the mid-fifties, notably the years 1956-8, when he was a prefect. Then he was at his peak. He had always, I'm sure, tyrannised over boys smaller than himself, but as a prefect he had real power. One of my waking nightmares is a memory picture taken through my legs as I was bent over for punishment: it is of Wicklow running forward, cane raised. The memory is terrible not just for the pain that came after – the sharp, annihilating pain, repeated over and over – but especially for the expression of unbounded relish on his face. After the first stroke he always laughed – the laugh succeeding his victim's first cry of pain, telling him, as if he didn't know already, that any pleas for mercy would be so much wasted breath.

Wicklow wasn't just physically cruel: he had a nice line in psychological torments too. The most perilous position at Manorfield was that of a new boy whom Wicklow apparently befriended. He could combine the psychological and the physical, as when he would overlook a minor offence with the chilling phrase: 'I'll save it up.' The end of this 'saving' was always a beating of horrible ferocity.

Now you will say: 'But this was the fifties. Things like that didn't happen then.' Oh, but they did: they happened in some 'good' schools, and they happened in many bad schools. Manorfield was a very bad school. I told my father what was going on when I went home for the holidays, but he just shrugged and said it was part of the process of growing up, that I needed to be

4

toughened up, that he wouldn't want people to say that any son of his was a ninny. I think his attitude was that *he'd* been through it in his time, so he didn't see why I shouldn't go through it in my turn. I think, even, that he rather enjoyed the thought. When, many years later, he begged me not to have him put in an old people's home I found it quite easy to harden my heart.

'Cardwell! If it isn't young Cardwell. Still got your nose buried in a book I see.'

His face was reflected, horribly distorted, in the wet bar-room table, a twisted version of my nightmare picture. My heart sinking, I looked up. There he was, standing over me as so often before: those rugby-player's shoulders, the large hands now clutching a pint glass, the beer belly, and above all the chilling smile. I nodded, casual, very cold, trying to disguise the fact that I still felt fear of him.

'Hello, Wicklow,' I said.

'You'd seen me, hadn't you? Recognised me. And you didn't come over to say hello.'

'Is there any reason why I should?'

'It would have been friendly. What are you having?'

I shook my head grimly and put my hand over my glass.

'Wise man. I'm going to have to try to get rid of this.' He patted his belly and went over to the bar. I sat there praying that was the end of the encounter, but knowing it was not. He brought his fresh pint over to my table and sat down. 'That wasn't friendly, you know, Cardwell,' he said, 'seeing me over there on my own and shrinking into your – whatever it is.' He waved his hand contemptuously at my periodical. 'But then you always were a cagey little sod. What's the word? Introverted, that's it.'

5

I tried to assert myself. 'Look, Wicklow, what is this about? I think I've made it pretty clear you're not welcome.'

'You haven't been chummy, but I can't for the life of me see why not.'

'If you're so thick that I have to spell it out, then I'll spell it out: you're not welcome because you're a sadist who made my schooldays a misery.'

'Good heavens, that was thirty years ago! What a time to nurse a grievance. Blame the system, blame the school.'

'The system allowed it, you took advantage of it. You were the most appalling bully.'

Wicklow smiled. 'I dispensed discipline.'

'You did a whole lot more than that. And you enjoyed it.'

'Of course I enjoyed it. It would have been a bloody silly waste of effort if I hadn't, wouldn't it?'

The frankness of the admission took me by surprise. He was beginning to fascinate more than repel me.

'You used to come back after you'd left—' I began.

'Oh boy, yes! I used to play with the First Fifteen when they just had friendlies. And then in the gym afterwards . . . I was in peak condition then. Though I say it myself, I was an artist. I had an agreement with the head boys who came after me. They used to save the hard cases for me to operate on. I used to look forward to those Saturdays . . . Hated it when they came to an end.'

Oh, the lovely English nostalgia for our schooldays.

'Yes, I remember my last two years were free of you,' I said.

'An old aunt, last of her line, running a small

6

manufacturing business, adopted me as her heir. I changed my name, took over the running of the business, moved up to Scotland.' He sighed. 'It was an offer I couldn't refuse, but there was some heart-searching, I can tell you.'

'I can imagine you running a business,' I said.

He laughed, that Wicklow laugh I remembered so well. 'You think I'm the sort of industrialist who lays off his workers just before Christmas, don't you?'

'Yes, Wicklow, I do.'

'Not at all. Nothing so crude.' His face twisted into the Wicklow smile. 'But I do have a list of birthdays and wedding anniversaries.'

'That figures,' I said. 'Are you married yourself?'

'I was, briefly. She couldn't stand the . . . pace.'

'You really are an appalling man, aren't you?'

'I am what I am what I am. Blame the school.'

'You didn't have to use the system in the way you did.'

'Good Lord, can you imagine anyone with my tastes *not*? And who's to say it wasn't the school, giving the older boys those powers, that nourished the tastes in me. You're not being logical, old man.'

'I'm not feeling logical.'

'Though to be fair, a sadist will always find an outlet, one way or another. Look at the language politicians use when the mortgage rate goes up: "hurt", "bite", "strong medicine". I'm not very different to thousands of others. You just had a few bad times, that's all.'

'You changed my whole character.'

He shrugged. 'You look to me to be a perfectly normal man. Of a certain type.'

'You really have no shame, have you?'

'None whatsoever. I've had a good life on the whole. Shame should be felt when you haven't done what you could have done, even though you wanted to. I've usually been able to do what I've wanted to do. The only thing I've never done is murder anyone.'

'You could murder my wife,' I said.

We both laughed. A shared bar-room joke that I despised myself for having initiated. But as I drained my glass my hand shook at having given myself away to him. He put out his hand and took my glass.

'You'll have that refill now, won't you? Dry white? It would be.'

By the time he returned from the bar I had got my breath back. The words had come out involuntarily because I was so preoccupied with what to do about Eileen. But I'd treated it as a joke, and he'd treated it as a joke.

'So what about you?' he said, settling his bulk down behind the table. 'What do you do for a living?'

'Oh, nothing very exciting. I work for Nicolls, the publishers.'

'Might have known it would be something bookish.'

'Actually I'm on the production side. Oh, they give me a manuscript to advise on now and again, something in my field, or something on one of my hobbies. But mostly the job is practical and financial. I come up here once a fortnight because our printing works is here.'

'Ah . . . But you live in London?'

'Yes. Or Bromley anyway. I commute, along with thousands of others.'

'Nice house?'

'Nice enough. Bromley isn't exactly Olde Worlde.

8

Still, it's big – bigger than we could afford if we were buying it now – and it's got plenty of ground. When you've been to boarding school you value privacy.'

'That's right. Children? I should think you'd like children.'

'No. My wife is . . . delicate.'

'Ah, shame. But you like your job, do you? It's satisfying, I should think.'

'Yes. Yes, it is that. I'd like to be on the editorial side, that's where my interest lies. But I'm too useful on the production things – I'm up in the technology, very good at costing, and so on. So I suppose that's where I'm stuck.'

'And the . . . special interest: where does she work?'

'I'm sorry—'

'Come off it, Jeff, we're both men of the world.' He laughed hugely, and I hated the thought of being a man of the world alongside him. 'You're either having something on the side, or there's a prospect in view.'

Inevitably I produced my man of the world credentials. 'Well, there is someone in publicity. A lot younger than me, but – well – she seems—'

'Interested. Good. Good for you! And hence your little matrimonial problem.' We both laughed. It was all a great laugh. 'But that shouldn't be a problem these days, should it? I got rid of mine – well, strictly speaking she flew the nest. Why shouldn't you do the same, or persuade your wife to?'

'I told you, she's delicate.' My smile was bitter. 'You've no idea how delicate a delicate wife can be. She spends half her life in bed. The fact is, her sanity's on a knife's edge.'

He raised his eyebrows and laughed heartily again.

9

'Guilt. That's your problem, isn't it, Jeff? You can't do what you want to because you would be consumed with guilt afterwards.'

'Yes. That is my problem.'

'As I say, I've never felt that way. Perhaps I am the man to help you with your . . . matrimonial problem.'

He said it with a huge smile, and I laughed back at him.

'What do you propose? Some kind of *Strangers on a Train* deal, where I do one for you in exchange?'

'Good Lord, no. If I wanted a murder done I wouldn't choose a wimp like you to do it.'

I was still laughing, but inside I cringed. What was it in me that wanted to live up to his horrible standards?

'No,' he went on, 'what I was proposing was a personal service to you. You obviously feel some kind of bitterness – God knows why, after all these years – and I'm proposing to make it up to you.'

'And achieve a personal ambition.'

'And achieve a personal ambition. So make sure when you're up here again on – when will that be? – the seventeenth—'

'That's right. The seventeenth and eighteenth.'

'—that you take someone out to dinner in the evening, make a late night of it, be at the works early in the morning, and go home again in the usual way. When would that be?'

'I catch a midday train, get home a bit after six.'

'There you are: problem solved.'

This was all done with great grins, lots of laughter – as if we were still schoolboys, and schoolboys who liked each other. But inside my heart was beating fast.

'Joke over,' I said. 'I love my wife.'

'Absolutely, old boy. All husbands do.'

10

'There is no matrimonial problem.'

'Quite. And you're getting younger every day, and the little thing in publicity will wait for ever. I get the picture . . . Christ, I need a pee.' He stood up, looming over me in the old way, looking down at me and smiling. 'Of course I'd make it look like a robbery.'

I sat there as he lumbered off to the lavatories, shouldering smaller drinkers aside. Half of me wanted to escape from him, from his threatening presence and from the hideous memories he evoked. The other half told me I had to stay, to make sure it *had* been a joke, to get the message through to him that if he had been serious he'd better think again because *of course* I didn't want him to murder my wife . . .

I sat, and sat, and sat. Wicklow did not return. His cruelty was as beautifully calculated as ever. After half an hour I went back to my hotel. It was an effort to behave normally as I collected my key at the desk. When I got to my room I ran into the bathroom and stood over the basin, retching, heaving, crying. As I lay on my bed afterwards, staring at the ceiling, I remembered times at school when I had done exactly the same thing after sessions with Wicklow. Same old Wicklow, same old Cardwell. And a situation that nothing at Manorfield School had prepared me for.

With daylight things didn't seem quite so bad. On the long train trip home I reasoned that of course he had not been serious: it had just been one of Wicklow's 'games' – those horrible playings with people that had been almost worse than the beatings. The whole thing had been the drama of an evening, something to enliven a chance encounter. True, the other half of me

11

said that one way or another I'd given him all the information he needed, and something very deep down said I'd given him the information because I wanted him to have it, wanted him to do what he was engaging himself to do. But on the whole I had convinced myself by the time I returned home that it was all a nightmarish joke, nothing more. I could face Eileen with my usual cheerful patience.

Two days later I received his postcard. *Definitely interested in that business arrangement. Cheers, Chris.*

I had forgotten his Christian name. Nobody thought of him as anything but Wicklow at school. A Christian name would have humanised him. The postcard was a view of Durham, and it was posted in Berwick. It was addressed to my home – he must have got my address from the telephone directory, the only Cardwell in Bromley. I thought of getting on to Directory Enquiries and asking for a C. Wicklow in Berwick, but then I remembered he'd changed his name.

'Any letters, Jeff?'

Wicklow needn't have bothered to be enigmatic on the card. Eileen was never down to breakfast. Often she never came down at all. It was a red letter day if she made it to the shops to get something for our dinner. Mostly we lived out of tins, and off prepared meals I bought at weekends and kept in the freezer.

'Only bills, darling.'

Two days after that, this time at work, I got another card: *Made all arrangements for our date? I have. Cheers, Chris.*

It was a picture of Dundee, posted in Bradford.

'I think I'd better take Peters and his wife out to dinner next time I go to Glasgow,' I said to Taylor in accounts.

'Why?' He flicked through his cards and peered at my entertainments account. 'It's only nine months since you dined him last.'

'It seems so unspontaneous to take him regularly every year in April. I think he's a bit discontented. He's a good man and we don't want to lose him.'

'Oh, very well. But make it fifteen months before you take him again.'

Nicolls, you will have gathered, is not an open-handed firm. I rang Peters and made the arrangements. If he was surprised he was too polite to show it.

I hoped, through all this, that I was behaving normally. Susan, sadly, was the one it was most difficult to be with. She is a sweet girl, and very receptive to other people's moods, especially mine.

The day before I was due to go up to Glasgow I received a last postcard: *It's as good as done. Best wishes, Chris.*

It was a picture of Piccadilly Circus, and posted in SW1. I burned it, as I had burned the other two.

The things I do at the printing works in Glasgow are regular and standard, and I hope I did them this time in a regular and standard way. The dinner with Peters was more difficult. I tried not to be too hectic in my joviality, spun the meal out longer than usual by insisting we had brandies with our coffee. I think Peters was surprised when I suggested a nightcap in the bar of my hotel. It was by then half past ten, and the last flight from Glasgow to London had just gone – still, you couldn't be too careful. The Peterses agreed to 'just a quick one,' and when they left I named a wrong room number at Reception to make sure I was remembered. Not that it was necessary: I was a regular there, known and liked. I, who was hoping that at that very time Wicklow was murdering my wife. Was I hoping? Or merely planning in case he did? I cannot now disentangle my conflicting feelings.

The next day I went early down to breakfast, early off to the works, where Peters informed me that he and his wife had thoroughly enjoyed their evening. By eleven the various chores were done, and I had coffee with several of the management in the canteen. Then I took a taxi to the station.

On the train I relaxed my guard a little – relaxed my face muscles, allowed myself to frown, got myself a gin and tonic from the buffet. I pretended to read my *Guardian*, took out my papers and did one or two calculations of costs. But there was only one thing on my mind.

I crossed London, took the electric train to Bromley, and walked home. It was by now well after six, and dark. There was no outside light on at my house, but then there often was not. I let myself in, turned on the hall and outside lights, and shouted up the stairs: 'I'm home darling.'

There was no reply. There usually was a reply, unless we'd had a tiff. I left my case in the hall, went into the living-room, where all was normal, then I went up the stairs. Heavily, reluctantly. There were no lights on, and everything was deathly still. Was I imagining it, or was there a smell – a terrible, insidious smell? I turned on the landing light, and then went to our bedroom door and turned on the light there.

The scene was terrible. She had known what was coming to her, but then I realised with a sickened shock that with Wicklow that would obviously have been part of the plan. The bed was terribly disturbed, and Eileen was lying across the foot of it in her nightdress, her throat cut, and her blood everywhere. I screamed in genuine horror, ran halfway down the stairs, was pulled up by a fit of retching from which nothing came up, then I ran down the remainder of the stairs and picked up the phone in the hall. Clumsily, feverishly, I dialled 999.

'Police! Quickly! My wife has been murdered! Please come! 25 Ravenscroft Avenue. Please! Please come!'

A patrol car was outside the house in five minutes, and in another minute or two a car with two detectives. I met them at the door, still ashen-faced and sobbing. They ran upstairs and I dragged myself up and stood on the landing, unable to look through the door, but bent against the wall, my forehead against the cool of it, sobbing, my stomach still heaving with disgust and fear.

'You've just got home, sir?' said the Detective Sergeant at the bedroom door. The three others came to join him there.

I nodded, swallowing. 'Yes. I've had two days in Glasgow, on business. She must have been killed last night while I was away.'

'Last night, sir? She's still warm. The blood hasn't dried. I'd say she hasn't been dead half an hour.'

'But that's impossible! He said—'

I raised my head and encountered the eyes of four policemen, looking at me with intense suspicion. I do not now know whether I heard, or simply seemed to hear, the familiar laugh of Wicklow from the garden.

False Scent

Simon Brett

False Scent

THE BODY OF FIFTY-FIVE-year-old Ralph Rudgwick was discovered by his wife, Jane, on the Sunday evening when she returned from a Weekend Water-colour Painting Course in the Lake District.

He was lying in a tangle of sheets in the overheated bedroom of their house near Henley, dressed only in a royal blue shirt, the front of which was plastered to his body with the brown blood that had spread from three bullet-holes in his chest.

His other clothes, Jane Rudgwick told Detective Inspector Bury, had been lying in an abandoned heap on the floor. She had hung up the trousers and aligned the shoes with his others in the wardrobe. The boxer shorts and socks she had placed in the dirty clothes basket.

When the Inspector asked her why she had done this before contacting the police, she seemed at a loss. 'Well,

I like to have everything tidy,' she had replied, puzzled by his question.

At first he had put the reaction down to shock. Discovering your husband murdered must be one of the most traumatic experiences in the life of any woman, and logical behaviour should perhaps not be expected at such a moment.

Anyway, at their first interview, it seemed incongruous to suspect anything sinister about Jane Rudgwick. She was a strange, vulnerable little woman, the wrong side of fifty, from whom all colour seemed slowly to have seeped away. Her face, and her flowered cotton dress, were as anaemically pastel as the decor of the obsessively neat sitting-room, in which they sat talking.

The eyes, blinking through transparent-framed glasses, were pink with crying, and she kept breaking down and rushing off to the bathroom to recover herself. From these sorties she would return with eyes redder than ever, and surrounded by a haze of cheap flowery perfume, as though she believed, pathetically, that that could cover up, or sanitise, or even dispel the ugliness that had invaded her life.

It was only when, the following morning, Detective Inspector Bury interviewed Jacob Keynes, Ralph Rudgwick's partner in the Keynes Rudgwick Gallery, that his suspicions began to move towards the dead man's wife.

The gallery was Cork Street smart, its narrow glass frontage dominated by a huge abstract oil in strident primary colours. The name of the painter, an unsolved anagram of Middle-European consonants, meant nothing to Detective Inspector Bury. But then he would never have claimed to know anything about art.

Jacob Keynes also favoured primary colours, a scarlet jacket of generous Italian cut over a yellow shirt and green trousers. His aftershave, an expensive, slightly sickly cologne, pervaded the atmosphere.

He seemed neither upset nor surprised by the news of his partner's murder.

'So the worm finally turned,' was his first comment.

'I'm sorry, Mr Keynes?' said Bury, urbanely unruffled, as his profession demanded. 'Could you amplify that remark a little?'

'Ah.' The gallery owner was struck by doubt. 'Well, perhaps I shouldn't . . .'

'I think, having gone that far, you *should*, Mr Keynes.'

'Yes . . . I'm obviously not making any accusation or anything like that—'

'Obviously not.'

'—but my first reaction to the news was, I'm afraid, to suspect Ralph's wife of killing him.'

'She being the worm you mentioned, the one who finally turned . . . ?'

'Yes.'

'Uh-huh. And do you have any reason for your suspicion – except for the obvious one that most murders prove to have domestic motivations?'

'I do have reasons, but I'm not sure that I should . . .'

'Once again, I think you absolutely *should*, Mr Keynes.'

'Right. Well, you'll find out soon enough from someone else if I don't tell you. Ralph was perhaps not the most faithful of husbands.'

'Ah. He had a lot of girlfriends?'

'Over the years there have been a few.'

21

'And do you think his wife knew about them?'

'I wouldn't know. Maybe not. None of them was very serious or lasted very long. However, recently . . .'

'Yes, Mr Keynes? Recently . . . ?' said Bury, deterring another attack of reticence.

'Recently Ralph had got into a more serious extramarital relationship.'

'Ah.'

'For the last – I don't know how long it's been – must be getting on for six months – he's had a mistress.'

'Really?'

'He has – *had* a flat in Covent Garden where he stayed two or three nights every week. When he's been in London over the last few months, he's spent most of his spare time with his mistress.'

'Could I have her name?'

'Gina. Gina Luccarini. She's Italian,' Jacob Keynes glossed unnecessarily. 'A painter. That's one of hers.'

The canvas he indicated was in similar style to the Middle-European anagram in the window. Bold swirls of bright colour. Angry. Slightly disturbing.

'Would you happen to know where Miss Luccarini lives?' asked the Inspector.

Jacob Keynes gave an address in Notting Hill. 'But you won't find her there at the moment.'

'Oh?'

'She's in Italy. Gone to visit her mother. Flew out at the weekend. Saturday, I think.'

'Hm. And, since Mr Rudgwick has been seeing Miss Luccarini, has he kept up with any of his other girlfriends? Or indeed picked up with any new ones?'

Jacob Keynes hooted with laughter. 'I can't see Gina tolerating that, Inspector. No, there's a rule with mistresses – particularly hot-blooded Italian mistresses – they can just about tolerate their man spending time with his wife – even, though this apparently wasn't the case with Ralph, making love to his wife – but if he starts anything else – anything extra-extramarital, as it were – then all hell's let loose. And Gina, I imagine, would be capable of letting loose quite a lot of hell.'

'Thank you, Mr Keynes,' said Detective Inspector Bury with a quiet smile. 'I'll bear that in mind. So . . . it is your belief that Ralph Rudgwick was very serious about Miss Luccarini?'

'Oh yes. He was in love with her, no doubt about it. And she with him. A very strong, passionate relationship. Ralph kept saying he would have moved in with her permanently – but for the fact that he was married.'

'Doesn't stop a lot of people these days, Mr Keynes. There is such a thing as divorce.'

'According to Ralph, Jane wouldn't hear of the idea. Anyway . . .' he gestured round the gallery, ' . . . Jane's money bought most of this, and Ralph didn't want to put his nice cosy set-up here at risk.'

'Doesn't that mean that Mr Rudgwick's death puts you in financial difficulties, Mr Keynes?'

The gallery owner favoured him with a patronising smile. 'No, Detective Inspector. Money has never been a problem for me. If I choose to replace Ralph, I will. And, if I don't . . .' he shrugged, ' . . . I'll just run the place on my own.'

Bury looked thoughtful. 'So . . . To recap . . . It is your assumption that Mrs Rudgwick killed her husband because she could no longer stand the humiliation of his flaunting his mistress at her?'

'Something like that, yes.'

'Did you ever see him actually humiliate his wife in public by appearing with his mistress?'

'No. But then Jane was never there on such occasions.'

'Oh?'

'Jane hardly ever came to London. She stayed down in Henley. And tried to keep Ralph down there as much as possible too.'

'How do you mean exactly?'

'She kept being ill, so he had to go back home rather than stay in London. Well, at least she claimed she was ill . . .'

'Meaning you don't think she was?'

'I think it was just her way of demanding his attention. Since she didn't have any sexual power over him, she had to exert some other kind of control. Money was part of it, but her health was always there to fall back on. I mean, the whole of the last fortnight, for instance, Jane claimed to be ill. Poor old Ralph was having to commute from Henley every day – even stay down there some days. No opportunity to see Gina for anything more than the odd meal – very frustrated he was getting.'

'And you think Mrs Rudgwick's illness was pure fabrication?'

'Well, the timing does seem a bit odd, doesn't it? She's so ill for two weeks that hubby has to go back home every night, but then when she wants to go off on her painting course – and when she knows that hubby's mistress is about to go to Italy for a fortnight – she suddenly gets better.'

'Hm.' The Inspector tapped his chin reflectively. 'And

did Ralph Rudgwick ever talk to you in detail about how unsatisfactory his marriage was?'

'Well, no. Not in so many words. But, come on, I didn't have to be Sherlock Holmes to deduce it from the circumstances, did I?'

'No,' said Detective Inspector Bury slowly. 'No, perhaps not.'

In the pastel sitting-room, Jane Rudgwick looked as puffy-eyed as ever at their next encounter, which took place on the Monday afternoon. Once again an invisible miasma of scent floated around her.

'So you drove up to the Lake District for your painting course, Mrs Rudgwick?'

'Yes.'

'Arriving there at ten o'clock in the evening.'

'Ah. You checked?'

'Yes, Mrs Rudgwick. Now, assuming Friday evening traffic, and assuming you drove up the M5 and M6—'

'Oh, but I didn't.'

'What?'

'I hate driving on motorways. All that traffic, all going so fast. No, I drove up through Cheltenham, Worcester, Shrewsbury and so on . . . All the minor roads.'

Well, that's in character for this little mouse of a woman, thought the Inspector as he observed out loud, 'Must've taken you a lot longer.'

'Yes, but it put less of a strain on my nerves.'

'Of course. So what time did you leave the house on the Friday?'

'About three.'

'And was your husband here when you left?'

'Yes. He hadn't gone into the office that day.'

'Why not?'

'I don't know, Inspector.' The puffy eyes blinked ingenuously through the glasses.

'And you didn't have any argument before he left?'

'Argument?' Jane Rudgwick echoed the word, as if it was in a foreign language she didn't speak. 'Me and Ralph? No.'

'Are you suggesting that you never argued?'

'We didn't have anything to argue about.'

Detective Inspector Bury let that pass for the moment. 'So, Mrs Rudgwick, would you say yours was a happy marriage?'

'Oh yes,' she replied, 'yes,' as if she were surprised that he had even thought to ask the question.

He changed tack. 'According to our records, Mrs Rudgwick, your husband owned a pistol.'

'He did, yes. He used to be quite keen on target shooting. Hadn't done it for a year or two, but in the past he did. Was a member of a club, that kind of thing.'

'Mm. The gun that killed him was similar to the one he owned . . .'

'Ah.' A sob welled up in Jane Rudgwick's throat at this reminder of the reality of her husband's death.

' . . . but we haven't been able to find his gun anywhere in the house.'

'I think he used to keep it locked in one of the desk drawers in his study.'

'We've looked there. No sign of it. We've looked everywhere.'

'Oh.' She appeared genuinely puzzled by this information.'

'On the other hand . . .' Detective Inspector Bury timed his *coup de théâtre* carefully ' . . . we have found

26

traces of gunshot residue particles on some tissues in a bag of rubbish.'

'What rubbish?'

'The rubbish that had been tied up in a plastic bag and placed in your dustbin, Mrs Rudgwick . . .'

'Oh.'

' . . . which would appear to have come from your bathroom.'

'Yes. Yes, it did. I emptied the waste-bin from the bathroom when I got in on Sunday.'

'After discovering your husband's body?'

'Yes.'

'And before contacting the police?'

She nodded again.

'Don't you think that's rather odd behaviour, Mrs Rudgwick?'

But again, the only reply she could give, in a wondering, almost childlike voice, was: 'Well, I like to have everything tidy.'

Detective Inspector Bury was silent in the car back to the station. He hadn't worked before with the Detective Sergeant who had been assigned to the case, and did not find the young man particularly congenial. Certainly not congenial enough to be elevated into any kind of Dr Watson confidant role.

How pleasant it would be, Bury thought wryly, always to work with the same sidekick, to have one of those sparky, joshing relationships between Inspector and Sergeant so beloved of crime novelists and television series. What a pity that real police duty rosters didn't work like that, and that only occasional coincidence would find him paired with the same assistant on two consecutive cases.

The thoughts that he kept to himself in the car ran on Jane Rudgwick. He had by now concluded that her naivety and the general pallor of her personality must be a front. Nobody could really be that wishy-washy.

But if she had killed her husband, she seemed to show little instinct for self-preservation. Bury had given her a good few opportunities to defend herself and she had taken none of them.

For example, he had pointed out that the soiled tissues from the dustbin did not correspond to any others found about the house. The boxes in her bathroom and bedroom contained plain white ones, while these had been coloured boutique tissues.

But Jane Rudgwick's reaction had not been to seize on this as proof that someone else had been in the house. All she said was that she hadn't looked closely at the contents of the bathroom waste-bin, just tidied it up automatically.

Again, when Detective Inspector Bury had reported that preliminary examination of her husband's corpse suggested he could have died any time on the Friday afternoon or evening, she had not hastened to assert an alibi about the time of her departure, nor offered specific details of the route she had taken for the Lake District.

And when he commented on the strangeness of her illness of the previous two weeks and the way it had suddenly got better on the Friday, her only response had been. 'Yes, that was odd, wasn't it?'

All these reactions were so unusual that Bury found himself unable to take them at face value. Nobody could be that naive. No wife could be so totally unaware of her own candidature as a murder suspect.

And, given what he had heard about the Rudgwicks' marriage from Jacob Keynes, Detective Inspector Bury felt sure that Jane Rudgwick was hiding something.

Back at the station, he managed to shake off his unwanted assistant by delegating some routine phone calls to the Detective Sergeant. When he reached his office, Bury discovered that there had been a call for him from Gina Luccarini. The number she had left was a London one, and his surmise that she had returned from Italy on the news of her lover's death was confirmed as soon as he got through to her.

'A friend told me. I came straight away. It is a tragedy!'

Her voice, heavily accented and operatic in its intensity, contained none of the crumbling weakness of Jane Rudgwick's grief. It was passionate and furious.

'She killed him! It is wicked. She is the – what you call – dog in the manger. Because she could not have him, she is determined no-one else shall.'

As he had done with Jacob Keynes, Detective Inspector Bury made her spell out who she was talking about.

'His wife, of course. Jane.' Gina Luccarini spoke as to a child. 'She is a monster!'

This description seemed so at odds with the faded, blinking, red-eyed figure with whom he had spent the afternoon, that Bury could not help asking, 'Have you ever actually met Mrs Rudgwick, Miss Luccarini?'

'Well, no. I only heard about her from Ralph – and that was enough! From the start of their marriage, she allow him no sex-life at all. She use her money to have power over him. She treat him like garbage!'

Again, this behaviour seemed grotesquely inappropriate to the image Jane Rudgwick presented to the world, but Bury knew well the impossibility of imagining the inside of a marriage. And he found that the increasing incongruity of casting Ralph's widow in the role of murderer had the perverse effect of intensifying rather than weakening his suspicions of her.

'I think we ought to meet, Miss Luccarini.'

'Of course. Please.'

'Would it be all right if I were to come and see you this evening?'

'Yes.'

'What time would be convenient?'

'It does not matter. As late as you like. You think I will have any chance of sleeping after what has happened?'

Everything about Gina was as vibrantly colourful as everything about Jane was drab. It was not hard to sympathise with Ralph Rudgwick's choice.

The sitting-room of her apartment in Notting Hill was painted deep red, the walls animated with her own explosive canvases. Bright printed fabrics drooped from the windows and were draped with random elegance across the furniture.

She was probably thirty-five, vivid in a dress of blood-red silk, which showed the full length of her black-stockinged legs. The red was picked up in heavy flamboyant earrings and on full lips. Her hair had the rich darkness of espresso coffee, and the same colour blazed with fury from her eyes.

Around her hung the musky sensuality of a perfume whose expense severely restricted the numbers of its users.

Just as Jane Rudgwick could be viewed almost as a parody of the boring, frigid, Anglo-Saxon wife, so Gina Luccarini was perfectly cast as the tempestuous, sexy, Latin mistress.

'When did you last see Ralph Rudgwick?' asked Detective Inspector Bury, after refusing offers of coffee or alcohol.

'We had lunch on Wednesday.'

'And – I hope you don't mind my asking – that was just lunch . . . ?'

'Yes. We had thought then that he would be coming here on Friday night – after his wife had gone off for her *Water- colour Course.*'

She deluged the last three words in contempt. 'Is not that typical of her – of Mrs Jane Rudgwick – that she should work on *Water-colours*! And of course she had no talent. She is just a *weekend painter*. Pale, drab, useless – and she killed my lover!'

This reminder of the facts of the case which, in Jane Rudgwick, would have prompted sobbing, seemed only to make Gina Luccarini angrier. She was the type whose grief manifested itself in an active, rather than a passive way.

'You described Mrs Rudgwick as "pale", Miss Luccarini, but I thought you said you'd never seen her . . . ?'

'I have not. But I have heard a great deal about her from her husband. I feel I know her – know every cell of her pathetic, bloodless body!'

'Yes, yes, I see,' said Bury, not quite sure of the correct response to these arias. 'But, as it turned out, you did not see Ralph Rudgwick on the Friday night . . . ?'

'No,' Gina Luccarini replied. 'No, I did not.'

'He was probably already dead by then . . .' the

Inspector mused, interested to see what reaction this deliberate insensitivity might provoke. 'Did he contact you on Friday?'

'No,' Gina replied through what, for the first time in their encounter, could have been a sob. She swept up a purple silk handkerchief from the arm of her chair and rubbed it brusquely against her face to cover the lapse.

'Presumably, Mr Rudgwick talked to you about his marriage?'

Gina Luccarini was once again fully combative as she replied, 'He told enough for me to know that it was a marriage only in name – that there was no love, no passion.'

'But he didn't go into detail?'

'No. It was not an interesting subject – not one that we wished to talk about more than we had to. We had more interesting things to do with our time.'

'Yes. Of course. It is true, though, is it not, that Mr Rudgwick wanted to live with you, but his wife wouldn't give him a divorce?'

'That is true. That is what he told me, yes.' Another gust of anger swept through Gina. 'She was a dreadful woman! She gave him no freedom at all. Two months ago, Ralph he has to go to Paris for an auction. He is going to take me. We will have wonderful, romantic two days. Then suddenly his wife – Jane – she say she want to go. Right at the last minute. Once again she spoil our pleasure.'

'Do you think she did that deliberately?'

'I think so. Why else so suddenly? She could not make Ralph happy herself, and she was determined nobody else would do so. She is, as I say, a monster!'

'So you have no doubt that she knew about your

relationship with her husband?'

'She must have known. Everyone knew. We make no secret. We go to restaurants, opera. We are a unit. I have keys to his flat, he has keys to my flat. Whenever Ralph is in London, we are together.'

'Of course, Mrs Rudgwick was very rarely in London.'

'No, but she still must know. She lives with the man. No woman can be so stupid and insensitive not to know.'

'Maybe not.' Bury was thoughtful for a moment. 'And how long had you and Mr Rudgwick been seeing each other?'

'We met at a private view. Five months ago. It was instant attraction, you know.'

'Yes. And, er, I hope you don't mind my asking this, Miss Luccarini . . . but do you know if Mr Rudgwick had had mistresses before you?'

After what Jacob Keynes had said on the subject, it had not occurred to Bury that Gina might find this suggestion insulting, but the tornado of reaction it prompted left him in no doubt that she did.

'What are you suggesting: that I am just one in a long line of – what you call – "totties"! That he just pick me up for a bit of sex! That it was not a serious relationship!'

'No, no, no.' The Inspector finally managed to calm her. 'I was just asking. I mean, he had been married for nearly twenty years. If his relationship with his wife was as unsuccessful as you've suggested, then it might not have been surprising if he'd looked elsewhere before he met you.'

'He did not!' she snapped. 'He met me, and for the

first time he knew what it was to be in love – to be really, fully in love!'

'I see.' Bury hesitated. 'Well, your reaction to that makes me think perhaps I shouldn't ask the next question I had in mind . . .'

'What was it?'

'I was going to ask whether you knew of any other girlfriends he was seeing while he was going around with you?'

Gina Luccarini's furious reaction proved that the Inspector's hesitancy about asking the question had been fully justified.

It was time, Detective Inspector Bury decided, for a bit of straight talking to Jane Rudgwick.

Her voice sounded strained when he rang her the next morning, but she was as co-operative as ever. No, she wasn't going out. Yes, he was welcome to come round whenever he wanted to.

Behind the spectacles, her eyes again looked very raw, as if she had been crying all night. And the pervasive flowery aroma which surrounded her made a sharp contrast to the exclusive perfume of Gina Luccarini.

Now that he could contrast the mistress and the wife, Bury had no difficulty in sympathising with – almost even condoning – Ralph Rudgwick's behaviour.

Vying with Jane's scent that morning, there was also a smell of furniture polish. He knew that the sitting-room had not just been done for his benefit, but that its cleaning was part of an obsessive daily ritual.

'So, how're things going?' asked Jane Rudgwick, her small talk incongruous in the circumstances.

'Our investigations are proceeding,' replied Bury, all policeman. 'My Sergeant's making local house-to-house enquiries, to check whether anyone saw anything unusual. And then forensic tests are continuing on various objects that were taken from the house, and, er . . . on your husband's body.'

'Oh. Oh.' A sob trembled through Jane Rudgwick. 'Excuse me . . .'

She rushed from the room. When she returned, her eyes were redder than ever, and it seemed as though she had drenched herself in scent.

'I'm sorry about that. It's still . . . a shock, you know . . . When you mention . . . you know . . .'

'Yes, of course . . .' Detective Inspector Bury soothed, lulling her into relaxation before his sudden change of approach.

'I want to talk about your husband's infidelity, Mrs Rudgwick,' he announced firmly.

'Oh.' She looked totally crestfallen. 'You knew about that?'

Bury nodded, but before he could say anything, Jane Rudgwick continued, pleadingly, 'It was only the once, though.'

'What?'

'Once. Only once that Ralph was unfaithful to me. In Paris.'

'In Paris?' Bury was too stupefied to do more than echo the words.

'Yes. A couple of months ago. Ralph told me all about it. He met this girl in his hotel, and they had a few drinks, and got talking and . . . well, one thing led to another. He was heartbroken about what had happened. He said he was completely in the wrong, and he swore it'd never happen again, and he said he'd fully understand if I turned him out, but . . . our relationship wasn't like that . . .'

'So what happened?' the Inspector asked dully.

'Well, I was hurt, obviously – it would be foolish for me to pretend otherwise – and my confidence was hit, but I think in some ways it turned out to be a good thing.'

'A good thing?'

'Yes, because it made us talk about our marriage. You know, if something works, you tend not to question it, you just let it tick over, and perhaps I had been getting to the stage of taking Ralph a bit for granted. I mean, the fact that he succumbed to the girl in Paris . . . well, maybe it meant there was something he wasn't getting from being married to me. So, anyway, we talked about it – talked about things in a way we hadn't since the days when we were first engaged – and I think, though I'm sorry for what caused it, that in a strange way it made our relationship stronger.'

'Ah.' Bury realised he was almost literally gaping, and recovered himself sufficiently to ask, 'Wasn't there some thought of you going on that trip to Paris with your husband?'

She looked at him in innocent puzzlement. 'No. It would have involved flying. Ralph knew I hated flying. He would never even have suggested it.'

'Oh.' The Inspector tried once again. 'And you really do believe that that was the only occasion in the course of your married life that your husband was unfaithful to you?'

'Of course,' she replied ingenuously. 'I was very lucky, because I know some men are dreadful when it comes to that kind of thing.'

'Yes,' said Bury slowly, 'yes. And – I hope you don't mind my asking – but your marriage, I mean the sexual side, was satisfactory . . .?'

For the first time since he had met her, some colour came into Jane Rudgwick's cheeks. 'Well, it always seemed so to me,' she replied rather coyly.

'Ah,' said Detective Inspector Bury, 'ah, well . . .'

And he began to invert everything he had ever thought about the case. They always said the wife was the last one to know. Ralph Rudgwick had peppered his married life with infidelities, and his wife Jane had never known about any of them. Not even about the *grand amour* that had come to her husband at the age of fifty-five.

But, as he thought about it, Bury began to wonder just how *grand* the *amour* had been. He had Gina Luccarini's word for it – and indeed that had been supported by Jacob Keynes – but, given the kind of character that was beginning to form in the Inspector's mind for Ralph Rudgwick, they had perhaps both been deluded. A man who was capable of telling wholesale lies to his wife would have little compunction about doing the same to his mistress.

Before he could sort through all the ramifications of his changed thinking, the telephone rang. Jane Rudgwick answered it.

'Yes. Yes, he is.' She held the receiver across. 'For you.'

It was the young Detective Sergeant, bumptiously pleased with himself. 'I've got something. Old lady at the end of the road, apparently spends all her days snooping through the net curtains at everyone's comings and goings.'

'What about her?' Bury asked, a little testily.

'Early Friday evening, she saw a red Golf GTi arrive at the Rudgwicks' house.'

'How long did it stay?'

'She doesn't know. It was getting dark and she left her vantage point soon after to cook her supper. But she definitely saw it arrive about half-past seven.'

'Hm. Well, that could be very useful information . . . *if* we happened to know someone who owns a red Golf GTi.'

'We do.' The Detective-Sergeant was now downright crowing. 'Gina Luccarini owns a red Golf GTi.'

'Ah,' said Bury. 'Does she?'

'But this is ridiculous!' Gina Luccarini protested. 'What makes you think that I would kill the one person I have ever really loved?'

'I'm not yet saying you did,' Detective Inspector Bury replied evenly. 'I'm just asking you to answer some questions which might clarify a few points.'

'Clarify a few points!' She threw her arms in the air. 'All right – ask me what you want to ask.'

She was dressed on this occasion in black trousers and a buttercup-yellow silk blouse. Huge yellow kite-shapes dangled from her ears. Her perfume was heady, almost soporific, in the enclosed space of the flat.

Bury clicked the ansaphone once again, rewound the tape and replayed it. A cultured, male voice oozed charm from the machine.

'Love, it's me. Look, for reasons that are too complicated to go into, I can't make it to your place tonight. But I've got to see you before you go to Rome – got to! So please

*come down here, as soon as you can. I'll be alone after
seven, and I'll explain everything then – promise. I can't
wait to see you. I love you and I want to kiss you all over.
See you very soon. Bye.'*

Bury switched the ansaphone off and again asked,
'Why didn't you tell me about that? Why didn't you tell
me you went down to Henley on Friday evening?'

Gina looked sulky as she reiterated, 'I just thought
it'd make things more complicated. I thought, since I
didn't see Ralph, it would be simpler to pretend I hadn't
been there.'

'But you must realise that it makes your behaviour
look extremely suspicious.'

'Yes, now I realise that, but at the time . . . I am a
person of passion, Inspector – if an Englishman can
understand such a concept! Often I act before I think.
When you ask me about Friday, I make a decision on –
what you call – the spur of the moment, and now I can
see it was the wrong decision.'

'I think I would agree with you there, Miss Luccarini.'

He let the silence hang between them. Small sounds
came from the other parts of the flat, where the young
Detective Sergeant and two uniformed constables were
going through the artist's belongings. She had given
permission for the search, but then refusing it would
only have increased their suspicions.

A detail came back to the Inspector, of how, the night
before, Gina had covered her confusion with a
handkerchief when asked directly if she'd heard from
Ralph on the Friday. Slowly, the case against her was
falling into place.

'The trouble is,' he went on, 'that wrong decision you

made means that you lied to me about Mr Rudgwick contacting you on the Friday. And if you lied to me about that "minor detail", it does make me wonder whether you were lying to me about anything else . . . ?'

'No! I was not! Everything else it is the truth!'

'So you're sticking to your story that you drove all the way down to Henley and didn't see him.'

'Yes. I get there. I knock on the door – there is no reply. I try the back door. Nothing.'

'Miss Luccarini, as I said, the forensic tests on the rubbish left in the Rudgwicks' bathroom found some boutique tissues of the kind that you use which show traces both of gunshot residue particles and of your rather distinctive perfume.'

'She must have planted them! Jane Rudgwick planted them. I have never been inside the house in Henley. I have keys for the flat in Covent Garden, but not for the house. I tell you, when I go there Friday at seven-thirty, I don't go inside. There is no reply from the house. Jane has already killed him!' she concluded on a spurt of anger.

'But why would she want to do that?'

'How many times do I have to answer the same questions! She did not want our happiness! She wanted to destroy it!'

'Miss Luccarini, I don't think Mrs Rudgwick even had any idea that you knew her husband.'

'But she must have done.'

'I think she thought she had a very happy marriage.'

'But how could she think that? After the things Ralph said to me about their marriage —'

'Yes, but he had reasons to say those things to you.'

'What kind of reasons?'

'Well, initially, to get you into bed with him.'

Her eyes blazed and she tensed forward. For a moment Bury thought she was actually going to slap him, but she managed to control herself.

'That is not true. Ours was a real relationship. Ralph and I loved each other.'

'I think you'd find Mrs Rudgwick would use exactly the same words.'

'But she was . . . she had . . .' Gina Luccarini's hands clenched and unclenched as articulacy deserted her. Then she shook her head and said softly, 'I come back to the same thing – why would I want to kill a man I love?'

'Perhaps if he'd betrayed you . . .?' Bury hazarded casually.

'But he did not betray me.'

'When he went to Paris two months ago, he went to bed with another woman.'

'What, with his wife? All right, maybe the hotel only had double beds. But, even in your peculiar, anaemic language, "going to bed with" does not mean the same as "making love to"!'

'Ralph Rudgwick *made love to* a woman he met in the hotel.'

For the first time, Gina Luccarini looked pale, paler even than the translucent Jane Rudgwick. 'I don't believe you. His wife was there, for God's sake!'

Bury shook his head. 'His wife was not there. He told you his wife would be with him, but there was never any question of her going.'

'But it was supposed to be our wonderful, romantic time together. You are talking nonsense. Why would he tell me his wife was going with him and so I could not go?'

41

'Perhaps because he had already made arrangements to meet this other woman in the hotel . . .?'

It took a moment for the implications of this to sink in, before the fury seized her. Her hands clawed at the bright print artfully draped over the arm of her chair, tearing through the thin fabric.

'No,' she moaned. 'No . . .'

Detective Inspector Bury pressed home his advantage. 'And I think – in spite of this wonderful acting performance you're giving me at the moment – you knew that. I think that's why you killed him. Ralph Rudgwick was very vain, proud of his conquests. And he made the mistake of telling you about the latest one. That's what signed his death warrant.'

He found himself echoing Jacob Keynes' words. 'You could cope with the idea of him with his wife, but the thought of Ralph Rudgwick cheating on you with another woman – that you couldn't tolerate. It reduced you to the level of just another in a sequence of purely physical relationships, another pick-up, another easy lay. And your pride wouldn't allow him to get away with that.'

She shook her head in a terrified, mesmerised way. Her full lips still shaped the word "No", but no sound emerged from them.

At that moment the Detective Sergeant appeared, beam- ing and cocky, in the doorway. In his hand was a dripping polythene bag, whose contents could be clearly seen.

'Taped on to the inside of the lavatory cistern, Inspector,' he announced. 'Oldest trick in the book.'

Gina Luccarini looked at the pistol and continued to mouth silently and helplessly. She no longer looked beautiful or sexy. She looked like a beached fish.

And the sweat of terror had soured the aroma of her expensive perfume.

Jane Rudgwick stood in the pale pink bathroom of the house in Henley and looked at herself in the mirror. She had taken off her glasses and her pale blue eyes looked clear and sparkling. The previous day they had been puffy and red, but a long night's sleep had healed them.

She found, after all the traumas of the previous weeks, she was finally beginning to relax.

The knowledge that Gina Luccarini was in prison, awaiting trial for the murder of Ralph Rudgwick, contributed significantly to Jane's feeling of security.

It hadn't really been so hard. All marriages are unknowable – that was the single fact that had made the whole thing possible.

The man who tells his mistress that his home life is terrible, that his wife is frigid and refuses to give him a divorce, is a stereotype of modern life.

As is the devoted wife at home, blithely unquestioning of her husband's fidelity, the little woman who is, in obedience to tradition, 'the last to know.'

All Jane Rudgwick had had to do was to play variations on those stereotypes.

The outline of her plan had been formed from the moment she found out about Ralph and Gina's relationship.

She had known about the other women, of course, but they had not worried her. Ralph had only gone with them for sex, an activity for which Jane had no feeling except a mild revulsion. The other women had at least deterred him from attempts to offload his restless libido on to her (though pretty early into their marriage he had given up any attempts in that direction). And the squalor of his furtive couplings had given Jane further ammunition with which to vilify her husband when she felt the need.

Because, of course, she had always been in control. Her money, and the threat of her withdrawing it from the Keynes Rudgwick Gallery, had always ensured that.

At one stage, when Ralph had been fulminating particularly violently against the trap into which she had incarcerated him, she had briefly worried that he might resort to murder to resolve the situation.

But she soon realised that he never would. Ralph Rudgwick didn't have that kind of strength in him.

Unlike his wife.

From the moment Gina Luccarini appeared on her husband's scene, Jane Rudgwick knew that she was different from the other women. This time there was more than sex involved.

And, instead of his customary shabby duplicities, this time he made no attempt to keep the relationship a secret from Jane. He told her everything about it, calmly announced that he wanted a divorce and, when she refused him that option, spoke seriously of getting out of the Keynes Rudgwick Gallery and trying something else.

It was this that had made Jane determined to teach him a lesson. Sexual jealousy was an alien concept to her, but she did deeply resent the idea of her husband finding happiness with someone else.

She decided that it was not just Ralph who should be taught a lesson. The woman who had had the effrontery to engage her husband's love should share in the punishment that Jane was preparing for him.

The idea of killing Ralph and having Gina convicted for the crime was so blissfully tidy that Jane Rudgwick hugged herself for days after she had thought of it.

The details were simple. It was really round the time of the Paris trip that the plan had crystallised. Jane knew her husband was intending to take his mistress on the jaunt, and she just had to choose her moment to announce that she herself wished to go. Ralph had remonstrated, but knew too well how Jane could make his proposed idyll a misery, so quickly caved in and put Gina off.

Jane had waited till they were actually at the airport before changing her mind. She knew by then it was too late for Ralph to salvage his previous arrangement with Gina.

Borrowing her husband's keys and getting Gina's copied had presented no problem. Nor had a trip to Notting Hill Gate on a day when she knew Gina to be out of town. A search of the flat had quickly revealed Miss Luccarini's tastes in tissues and perfume, as well as allowing Jane to reconnoitre a suitable hiding-place for the pistol when the appropriate moment came.

All that was required then was a fortnight of bullying, blackmail and generally bad behaviour in the run-up to Gina's departure for Rome. The only risk at that stage had been that Jane really would frighten her husband off, make him act on his oft-spoken intention to cut loose and move in with his mistress.

But Jane Rudgwick knew the man's fundamental weakness, and her judgement of his character had proved to be correct. He had fretted and whinged, but stayed around.

Getting him to invite Gina to Henley had been a

45

potential problem, but in the event easily negotiated. It was the threat of Jane not going on her Water-colour Course and thus preventing him from seeing his mistress at all before her departure for Rome that had clinched it.

Suddenly, mid-afternoon on the Friday, Jane had announced that yes, she felt better and she *was* going on the course, but she was worried about what Ralph might get up to in her absence, so she would stop every hour or so to phone and check up on him.

A man with any real character would have ignored this, but Ralph was very weak. He still hoped to find some solution to his situation that would combine having Gina with retaining his position in the Keynes Rudgwick Gallery set-up. For that reason he wanted to keep Jane sweet (or at least as sweet as she ever got).

So his only way out had been to do as he had done for most of his married life, and go along with what his wife said.

Jane had timed the announcement that she really was going to the Lake District very carefully. Her rival, she knew, tended to go out to a gym every afternoon between half-past three and five. By choosing quarter-past three as the moment to unleash her decision, Jane was certain that Ralph would try to contact Gina as soon as possible to let her know the change of plan.

She had waited outside his study door until she heard him leave the inevitable message.

Then all she had to do was to tell him to go upstairs to fetch her bag and, once he was in the bedroom, shoot him with his own gun.

That was the bit she had really enjoyed. Three

wonderfully satisfying tugs at the trigger. And, on her husband's face, a very rewarding expression of surprise giving way, first to terror, and then to oblivion.

She had wiped the gun on some of Gina's tissues, already impregnated with the artist's perfume, and thrown them into the bathroom waste-bin.

She had turned up the thermostat in the bedroom, having read somewhere that an overheated environment could make it more difficult to establish the exact time of a corpse's death.

Then she had driven up to Notting Hill Gate. She had time. The difference between the journey to the Lake District by the back routes she said was using and the motorways she really intended to use was considerable.

She watched her rival leave the apartment block on the abortive journey to Henley, slipped inside the flat, planted the murder weapon in the cistern, and then set off in her car for the motorways leading north.

A pleasant weekend's watercolouring, and back to Henley on the Sunday evening.

Yes, thought Jane Rudgwick, it really has all been very satisfactory.

Soon I'll be able to relax completely. But not quite yet. Still have to keep up the appearance of the grieving widow. You never know who might be watching.

So Jane Rudgwick picked up her atomiser of cheap scent and, bracing herself for the pain, once again sprayed it into her open eyes.

Good Old Monty

Michael Gilbert

Good Old Monty

JONATHAN AND SEBASTIAN WERE TWO hopeful young sharks. The sea they swam in stretched from Temple Bar to Aldgate Pump. It was full of reefs and pits, and currents which set in unexpected directions, and there were other sharks cruising about in it, older, heavier and more savage. So far they had managed to survive.

They had started with £5,000 each, the gift, in both cases, of aunts who had left it to them by will, coupled with the expression of a hope that they would put it to good use. The aunts were both believing Christians and it is possible that their idea of good differed from that of their nephews.

This joint fighting fund had grown over the past two years, more as a result of luck than judgement, or perhaps a little of both. They had stagged the Bryanstone issue, and had got into and out of International Cables at exactly the right moment. They had lost money in the Planetarium Project, but more than recovered it in Moon Stores when the shares nearly doubled in value as the result of a takeover bid by their largest rivals. They now had almost £100,000 waiting in a high interest deposit account.

'Ripe and ready for action,' said Jonathan.

'But where do we go in?' said Sebastian. 'The market's pretty dull at the moment.'

'We might devote a little attention to Office Accessories and B.T.'

'B.T.?'

'Business Tabulators.'

'Oh, that lot,' said Sebastian. 'What's so special about them?'

This was always the way. The more Jonathan got worked up the more laid back Sebastian became. Jack Sprat and his wife.

'The successful business man,' said Jonathan, 'spends perhaps ten hours in his office every day and the other fourteen at home – but most of that is sleeping and eating—'

'And commuting.'

'Yes. And commuting. Well, that doesn't leave more than, say, a couple of hours to fill in, if that. So what does he really need. An armchair, a television set and a comfortable bed.'

'And a comfortable wife.'

'Certainly. But think what a lot of attractive accessories he can buy to brighten up those ten hours in his office. The modern business man doesn't just need a massive desk and a well-adjusted chair—'

'What he really needs is a well-adjusted secretary.'

Jonathan ignored this. He was up in the stratosphere.

'He can have a computer of his own, with a Visual Display Unit. And if he finds it tiresome to read, he fits a moniscope which enlarges the text and brings it down onto his desk. He can have pocket calculators and desk top calculators, a digital diary and a data bank. His secretary can be equipped with a fax machine, a word processor or, failing that, an electric typewriter.'

'Do you ever see an ordinary typewriter these days?'

'You might find one in the V and A. And think of this. He can have a multi-lingual electric translator. If he wants to know what a Preference Share or a Debenture is in, say, Dutch or Arabic he just presses the button.'

'Stupendous,' said Sebastian. 'So what?'

'So we think very seriously about Office Accessories and B.T. Leaders in the field, and running neck and neck.'

'Cutting each other's throats.'

'Exactly.'

'Then why don't they amalgamate?'

'You took the words out of my mouth.' Jonathan had the Stock Exchange Year Book open. He said, 'Nominal Capital, in both cases, five million. B.T. two million Ordinary issued and subscribed. One million Preference.'

'*Preferente aandelen.*'

'What are you talking about?'

'Just showing you that I knew the Dutch for Preference Shares.'

'Keep your eye on the ball, please. Office Accessories much the same. One million five hundred thousand Ordinary. No Preference.'

'So,' said Sebastian, who really had been attending, 'since both shares are standing a few points above par,

53

either of them could take over the other *without increasing their Nominal Capital*. Their fingers must be itching.'

'Right. But *which* lot of fingers are itching most?'

The two young men looked at each other. The single table, at which they sat at opposite sides, and the floor round it were thick with copies of the *Financial Times*, which was the only newspaper they read.

'They're both holding their cards pretty close to their chests,' said Jonathan. 'You notice that they've neither of them published interim accounts. Maybe they're shy about this year's results.'

'It could have been a tough year,' agreed Sebastian. 'Eighteen months ago offices in the City were full of young men sitting on their bottoms all day fiddling with computers. That was when everyone was making money. Not now. Now a lot of them are on the street.'

'Right. And the last thing their company wants is more expensive office machinery. All the same, given good salesmanship they could have made a lot of money with those fancy lines.'

'We'll know as soon as the annual accounts are published.'

'No good. We must know sooner. When everyone knows it will be too late to do anything effective.'

'Do you think your Miranda might be able to help us?'

'For God's sake,' said Jonathan, 'she's only a typist at Accessories. Not the boss's right hand girl.'

'All the same she must know if they're getting keyed up for the A.G.M.'

Both companies were legally obliged to hold their Annual General Meetings before the end of October.

They would, no doubt, delay them as long as possible, but the Companies Act compelled them to give their shareholders at least twenty-one days' notice, along with the accounts and, in most cases, a statement by the Chairman.

'What we really want,' said Sebastian, 'is a reliable crystal ball. Failing that, I'll get round and make a few enquiries. You lush up Miranda and see if she can help.'

Jonathan accordingly spent his evenings standing Miranda expensive dinners whilst Sebastian passed his lunch hours in Panto's Sandwich Bar, off Cannon Street; where, if you listened hard, you could pick up more information about companies than you could on the floor of the Stock Exchange.

They met three days later to pool their information.

'I haven't got a lot out of Miranda,' said Jonathan. 'She's quite willing to help, but at the moment all she gets is general office gossip. One straw in the wind. There's been no announcement about the annual bonus. So maybe things aren't so good. But here's a gleam of sunshine. The boss's regular secretary has been ordered off work by her medico. She goes at the end of the week and it's been suggested that Miranda might stand in for her. It doesn't mean that she'll get anything top secret, but she's bound to pick up a few valuable crumbs.'

'Sounds hopeful,' said Sebastian. 'I've been concentrating on the managements. B.T. has got what you might call a run-of-the-mill board. All been at the job for a long time. Maybe too long. Accessories is quite different. A number of young directors and a couple of real packy-whatsits at the top.'

'I fancy the word you were looking for is pachyderms. But go on. This is interesting.'

55

'The Chairman is Colonel Melhuish. His number two is Major Messenger. The tone of the outfit is strictly regimental. They actually address each other as "Colonel" and "Major".'

'They can't be as old as all that.'

'Melhuish just scraped in, in the last months of the war. He was one of Montgomery's liaison officers. They both reached their present ranks in the T.A. That doesn't worry them. No, sir. For them the war is still on. If any important decision has to be made, the question is, *"What would Monty have done?"* '

'For Christ's sake,' said Jonathan. Like all young men he despised the generation ahead of him. That someone old enough to have been his grandfather was still active in the City was a joke, in rather poor taste. 'So what do the rest of the board do?'

'Search me. Actually they're quite a bright crowd. One of them's got a Harvard business degree, one was in furniture design and two started in International Electronics. But the point is that they're junior officers. Their job is to say, "Yes, sir. No, sir", and stand up when spoken to.'

'It doesn't sound to me like the sort of board to cope with a real crisis. And we don't want to guess wrong.'

Their experience with Moon Stores had taught them the facts of City life. The immediate result of a takeover bid being announced was always the same. The shares of the to-be-taken over company went up. The shares of the taker-over went down.

'Only temporarily, of course,' said Jonathan. 'If the taker-over is big enough to swallow and digest the smaller company, its shares will go up again. Maybe right up. But not until it's shown that it hasn't bitten off

56

more than it can chew.'

'I once saw a photograph,' said Sebastian, 'of a boa constrictor who'd swallowed a goat. He'd got it half-way down and he looked *most* uncomfortable.'

Jonathan was too deep in his own thoughts to worry about boa constrictors.

He said, 'The first step, clearly, is to put our money into Accessories. If they really have had a bad year, so much the better. They'll be ripe for being taken over. The shares will shoot up and we can sell when we think they are at the top. On the other hand, if we were wrong and they've been doing well, then they'll be the takers-over and we get out like lightning, before they've begun to dip.'

'Aren't you forgetting,' said Sebastian coldly, 'that there's another player in the game? The Stock Exchange. They'll have been thinking on exactly the same lines as us and they'll see the accounts as soon as we do. The Share and Loan Department will mark the shares down, as a precaution, *before the market opens.* What we've got to do is find out about those accounts in advance. How are we going to do that?'

'Keep our fingers crossed,' said Jonathan, 'and wait.'

They did not have to wait long.

It was Miranda who brought the news. She said, 'You wanted to know about those accounts, didn't you?'

'We certainly did.'

'Well, they've been arguing about them all week.'

'About what's in them?' said Jonathan hopefully.

'No. About who's to print them. I heard it all, because I'm now in what they call the Orderly Room. It's a tiny place, behind their office. I wonder why they call it that. Do you suppose it's a hint to me to keep it tidy?'

'It's a military term,' said Jonathan. 'Tell us about the printing.'

'Well, our printing's usually done by a small outfit called Williams and Davy. They hang out in Cork Street, off Bunhill Row. I had to take them a letter once and Mr Davy showed me round. They've got about half a dozen men working in the print shop. One old boy who looked as if he'd been there since the Boer War. The others were a lot younger.'

'And the argument was whether they could be trusted to handle the accounts?'

'Right. They'd always done them before, but Mr Messenger – the Major, that is – wanted them to go, this time, to a firm of security printers – whatever that means.'

'People who print share certificates and warrants and things like that. Very efficient and totally secure.'

'The Colonel said no, stick to the old firm. Apparently that was something General Montgomery had taught him. Don't desert your old friends just because someone more flashy turns up. But, he said, we'll make sure Davy understands how important security is. He must give the whole job to one reliable man. Me, I didn't see how he could do that. He'd have to print two thousand copies. Surely that would involve a lot of different people.'

'In the old days, perhaps,' said Jonathan thoughtfully. 'Not now. Not necessarily. Did you get any idea who might be given the actual job?'

'If I'd had to guess, I'd have said the old boy who sat by himself in the corner. He was almost buried under different machines. Only thing is, I wouldn't have put him in the top class for discretion.'

'Oh. Why not?'

'I thought he had a real drinker's face. Red nose, rum buds and all.'

'You can't always go by the colour of the nose,' said Jonathan. He spoke absently. His thoughts were far ahead.

He said, 'Here's where we need professional help. Smedley's the best man.'

Five days later Captain Smedley, who was the head of Temple Bar Detectives, gave Jonathan a verbal report. He said, 'The man you had your eye on is a Herbert Warburton. He's an experienced operator and, yes, he could do the job single-handed. He'd be given a handwritten copy of the Report and Accounts. He'd have a laser printer, a terminal with a keyboard and an NP 402 photocopier. He'd type the stuff out on the keyboard. The tape would be fed into the laser printer which would produce four pages of A4. They'd be separate pages, but no problem. When they're put through the photocopier it will turn out the necessary numbers of folded four page documents. The envelopes are ready. He puts them in himself and takes them down to one of the big central post offices. They'd be on everyone's tables at breakfast time next morning.'

Jonathan thought about it, prodding it to see whether there were any holes in it. He said, 'I suppose a copy would be kept in the office.'

'Possibly. In the boss's safe. But his instructions to Warburton would be to put the manuscript copy through the shredder and to wipe the tape.'

It seemed foolproof. As long as Warburton played the game.

As though reading his thoughts Captain Smedley said, 'Yes, we thought about that. My men kept

Warburton under observation for three days. His nose was a misleading signal. He turned out to be a teetotaller. He spent a good deal of time in milk bars and soft-drinks establishments. I began to get complaints from my men. Not the sort of place they normally frequent. So, having fallen down there, we made tentative approaches to one of the younger men, a youth who had been made redundant and was working out his notice. He was quite willing to help – at a price – but we soon discovered that he knew nothing about this particular job and the precautions being taken made it most unlikely that he'd be able to find anything out. So we reverted to Warburton. He had seemed unpromising, however—'

'However,' said Jonathan hopefully.

'Alcoholism isn't man's only vice. Warburton, it appears, is a gambler. Horses and dogs. As it happened both my men were on the job yesterday evening – one was relieving the other – at the moment when Warburton came out. A car drove up, he was bundled into it and driven off. My men followed discreetly. The chase ended in a quiet side street near the Oval. Warburton was dumped on the pavement and sat there, looking dazed. My men saw their chance. As soon as the other men – bookmakers' bullies they reckoned – had driven off, they picked up Warburton and whisked him into the back room of a nearby pub. He may have been a teetotaller, but when he was offered a large glass of brandy, he downed it like a man. From which point the entente developed quickly. It was what they had thought. He was nearly £800 in debt to his bookmaker and had just had a first warning of what to expect if he didn't pay up. When he was asked if he could get hold of a copy of the Report and Accounts some days in advance and if he would hand them over for a thousand smackers, in cash, he couldn't say "yes" quick enough.'

'A thousand,' said Sebastian thoughtfully when he was told. 'And we've got Smedley's bill as well. That'll be at least another five hundred.'

'Worth it,' said Jonathan. 'If we can once get a preview of the accounts we're sitting pretty. If they're bad, and suggest a takeover by B.T. our shares go up. If they're good, we can get out bloody quick, before they start angling for B.T. and their shares go down.'

'And when they have gone down, we can buy in again.'

'If the takeover looks like working.'

'All right,' said Sebastian. 'Green light for Captain Smedley.'

When, two days later, a smudged but legible copy of the Report and Accounts arrived, their message came over loud and clear. A nasty loss on trading, covered by a transfer from reserves which weakened a weak balance sheet still further. The Chairman's report was a cry for help.

'Lovely,' said Jonathan. 'As soon as B.T. read this they'll start making takeover noises and Accessories' shares go up. Every point they go up is a thousand pounds in our pocket. We must give Miranda a very special dinner.'

'You, not me,' said Sebastian. 'I've got to lush up my girl for a change. She's been complaining of lack of attention lately.'

Miranda had brought one other item of news. The A.G.M. had been fixed for October 28th. 'That means the accounts must go out tomorrow evening,' said Jonathan. 'Just the right moment for a celebration.'

They celebrated over an expensive dinner and continued the celebration in Jonathan's flat. Miranda was as satisfactory as a bed mate as she had been as a spy.

Jonathan had rolled over and was settling himself for sleep when she said, 'I forgot to tell you. A funny thing happened when I was leaving the office this evening.'

'Wassat?' said Jonathan sleepily.

'I'd left my bag behind and I nipped back to fetch it. The Colonel's office was empty. I went through it, to my little cubby-hole, picked up the bag and was starting back when I heard the two old boys coming. The Colonel must have gone along to have a word with the Major – his office is just down the passage. They were both laughing as they came along. The Colonel said, ''That was a real minor operation,'' and the Major said, ''It was terrific—'' and then they saw me.'

When she stopped, Jonathan, who had only half been listening, sat up in bed. He said, 'Go on. What happened?'

'Nothing actually happened. It was the look on the Colonel's face. As if he'd caught a spy and was going to have him shot. I was scared, for a moment. Then, thank God, I heard old Mrs Parkin rattling her pail and brushes. I said, ''Good night,'' and made for the door. Neither of them said a word. They just looked at me.'

Jonathan said, 'Let's have it again. Exactly what the Colonel said.'

'He said, ''That was a real minor operation.'' The Major agreed with him. It was what they were laughing so much about. They were both terrifically bucked – until they saw me.'

'Until they saw you,' said Jonathan slowly. 'Well, whatever it meant, we can't do any more about it tonight. Go to sleep.'

Miranda may have slept. Jonathan stayed awake until the first grey light of morning was creeping into the room. He dozed for an hour then.

Miranda cooked breakfast. Whilst they were eating it, she said, 'I don't really want to go back to the office.'

'You must,' said Jonathan. 'If you stay away they'll know you heard something you shouldn't have done. There'll be other people about. They won't start anything.'

His own office hours were irregular. He thought he'd take a walk and do some solid thinking. Not a walk in the country, with cows and road-hogs. A walk in the City among sensible people who thought about money. Bishopsgate, Houndsditch, Aldgate, Fenchurch Street, Lombard Street, Threadneedle Street.

Think, boy, think.

What was meant by a minor operation and why had the Colonel spoken about it in the way he did? Surely it would have been more natural for him to have said, 'It was *only* a minor operation, but it was successful.' Instead, they had referred to it as though it was a major operation.

Halfway down Aldgate he started thinking about 'minor'. Might it have been 'miner'? A digging operation. It opened a new line of thought, but didn't take him very far. Opposite the Bank of England a rather disturbing thought occurred to him. Might it have been a 'mina' operation. A mina bird, he remembered, could be taught to talk and repeat things back. Had they been using Miranda as a mina bird, telling her things which they knew she'd repeat? This was such an alarming idea that he quickened his pace and went round the whole circuit again, finishing outside his own office, two rooms on a top floor in Alderman's Walk.

Sebastian had left a note, *Off with Jeannie tonight. Great hopes.* He knew exactly what Sebastian was hoping for. Jeannie was a Scots girl with a dour character and a beautiful body. He wished him good luck, relocked the office and made for a restaurant where he could find a good high tea. By six o'clock he was home, sitting in his untidy living room, still thinking.

He decided to approach the problem from a different angle.

So far he had been wondering what the Colonel had meant and why it had seemed to him to be important. All right. Now, for a change, try to work out why it had seemed so significant to him, Jonathan. As it had done. It had made him sit up in bed. It had rung a bell. Something he had read somewhere.

This thought narrowed the field dramatically because, apart from the Stock Exchange Year Book, he didn't read a lot. Lately it had been books about the war. Not the 1939-45 War. His father and his uncle had bored him stiff yacking about that. No. The First World War. And not the war in the trenches, which had been a bloody shambles, but some of the interesting and picturesque outside shows.

Lights were springing up all round. You're on the right track now. Keep thinking.

He got up and looked at the clutter of books in the shelf beside the fire. And, by God, there it was. In front of his eyes.

He grabbed the book, leafed through the index to the letter 'M', turned back to the passage indicated and read it through. He had found what the Colonel was talking about. Then the reality of the position hit him.

It was seven o'clock. The Stock Exchange had long shut up shop. Impossible to sell today and tomorrow would be too late. He had found the answer and was powerless to use it.

Being given to extravagant gestures he was on the point of relieving his fury and frustration by hurling the book through the window when another thought occurred to him. Perhaps it was not too late. Accessories' shares were quoted on both the London and the New York Stock Exchange. If he was going to do it, he would have to be quick. No chance of consulting Sebastian. He would have to take the full responsibility.

He grabbed the telephone and started to dial.

On the following morning he reached the office at ten o'clock, beating Sebastian by a short head. Sebastian's face was as red as if it had been slapped. He was carrying two lots of papers, which he slammed down on the desk.

He said, 'In case you're interested, those are the accounts of Accessories and B.T. Both arrived this morning.'

Jonathan toyed with the documents for a moment, but made no attempt to read them.

'Go on. Help yourself to an eyeful. Accessories on top of the world. Good trading results, excellent reserves. B.T. on its uppers, almost begging to be taken over. And we paid that old shit Warburton a thousand smackers for a phoney set of accounts.' The thought seemed to choke him. 'All we can do is see if we can offload our Accessories' shares before they go down too far. Well, don't sit there like a bloody idol, say something.'

'I was waiting till you'd finished,' said Jonathan placidly. 'There's one excellent reason why we can't sell Accessories. I sold the whole lot yesterday evening through New York. They were actually a bit up on what we paid for them. Not quite enough to cover our expenses, but nearly.'

Sebastian stared at him.

'I realised, at the last moment, what the Colonel was talking about. It was a Meiner operation. M-e-i-n-e-r. Short for Meinertzhagen, who was on Allenby's Intelligence Staff in the Palestine Campaign. T.E. Lawrence actually refers to him in that way in *The Seven Pillars of Wisdom*. Look. *Meiner thought out false papers, elaborate and confidential*. That was what I'd read and it must have stuck in my mind. Allenby wanted to persuade the Turks that he was going to attack on the left, while actually he was going in on the right. So Meinertzhagen rode out between the lines, was spotted, turned tail and bolted. Carefully dropping his haversack in the process. Full of misleading information. Exactly what they pulled on us. A Meiner operation.'

Sebastian let out his breath in one long whistle.

'Thank the Lord you spotted it in time,' he said. 'This calls for a celebration. I'll book a table for four at the Savoy.'

'From which I gather,' said Jonathan, 'that you, too, had a successful evening.'

The Colonel and the Major were also celebrating.

'Jolly good show,' said the Colonel.

'A real haversack ruse,' said the Major. 'Monty did the same thing before Alamein.'

'That chap Warburton must have made a fortune. I wonder how many times he sold those phoney accounts. Almost everyone who was interested seems to have got their hands on them.'

'I believe he was asking a thousand a time at the end.'

'Effective, anyway. Stopped any last minute selling.'

'I believe one small packet was sold, in New York.'

'You know what Monty said. You can't trust the Yanks.'

'Good old Monty.'

There's an Explanation for Everything

H.R.F. Keating

There's an Explanation for Everything

MR MARTYN SHELBRAKE – HE LIKED to wear a plum-coloured waistcoat – would often announce that he was 'a product of the Scientific Age'. Even more often he would declare, with a touch of firmness, it was his belief that 'there's an explanation for everything'.

There was an explanation for his unusual Christian name. It was an eighteenth-century variant of the now more common spelling. There was an explanation, too, for his surname. He was a descendant 'of the Warwickshire Shelbrakes'. There was an explanation, equally, for why he had failed to perpetuate his branch of that once illustrious family. 'My dear fellow, if I had married and had had progeny, do you think I should have been able to live in the house I chose all of thirty-five years ago?' Mr Shelbrake's house was rather large, and very pleasant, in a quiet part of West London where aged and leafy plane trees gave shade in summer and delicately elegant bare-branched beauty in winter. 'And do you know, there's an explanation for the London plane tree. It's a hybrid, *platanus acerifolia*, the only variety that will truly tolerate a sooty environment.'

In point of fact Mr Shelbrake, who had sold at a good price the firm he had inherited from his father, a wine merchant – 'There's an explanation for that. We Shelbrakes have always been noted for our particularly discriminating palates' – devoted almost all his time to finding explanations and to telling other people what they were. He was seldom, very seldom, at a loss. True, when his next-door neighbour, E.L. Ridge, the author, once challenged him to say what explanation he had for so often wearing a plum-coloured waistcoat he had brushed the query aside with some asperity.

But that could have been because the two of them from the first days of their acquaintance had always been somewhat at odds. It was not that they quarrelled; it was that they bickered. The books from which E.L. Ridge derived the healthy income which enabled him, as a bachelor, to live in just such another house as Mr Shelbrake's, but more crammed if possible with valuable objects, were living contradictions of Mr Shelbrake's most cherished belief. They had titles such as *Mysteries of Time and Space* and *Mysteries of Seas and Oceans* or *Mysteries of Snowlands and Icelands*. And not one of them ever offered any explanation for any of the mysteries they described in their resonant and echoing prose.

Whereas Mr Shelbrake's occasional sorties into print

had been confined to some precise essays offering explanations for a few of the choicest unsolved murder mysteries. Unexplained crimes were a subject that had naturally attracted him once one of them had happened to come to his attention. So over the years he had claimed, contrary to most published evidence, that William Herbert Wallace was guilty of murdering his wife because when he had entered the dark curtained room where her body lay he had gone round to the far side to light the gas-jet thus indicating he knew just where the corpse was. He had an explanation, too, for believing that John Vinnicum Morse and not Lizzie Borden had been responsible for dealing out to her parents twenty-nine fatal whacks with an axe. 'Not forty, as in the rhyme. The explanation for that is that forty just scans better.' He had contended, too, that in Liverpool in the year 1889 the American Mrs Maybrick had soaked arsenic from fly-papers to deal, not with her husband, but with 'an eruption' on her face.

Such explanations for events safely in the past would have got Mr Shelbrake into no trouble, except perhaps for receiving a sharp printed rebuke from some expert in criminology. But, sadly, his ineradicable tendency to try to account for anything that happened to catch his eye drew him eventually to devote his attention to more immediate illegal activities than crimes safely in the past.

On his way home from his customary post-luncheon stroll one day – 'Walking soothes the digestion. There's an explanation for that. The flow of blood to the walls of the stomach is increased by gentle exercise' – he saw for a second time that afternoon a battered-looking van standing with its back doors wide and invitingly open while its driver, a decidedly rough-looking individual, sat sullenly slumped over the wheel. It was parked just at the exit of a narrow passageway that ran between the large gardens of the houses in two long parallel streets. Puzzling over the reason for the van being there so long, Mr Shelbrake eventually worked out that it must be because quite soon a smash-and-grab team who had operated at a bank or jeweller's shop in the nearby High Street would abandon their getaway vehicle at the far end of the passageway, run down it clutching their booty, leap into the back of the van and thus evade any pursuit.

As soon as he got indoors he telephoned the police. Only to find himself telephoned back half an hour later saying they were completely satisfied with the van driver's statement that he had been fast asleep all the time.

However, the somewhat icy tone in which he had been given that answer did not give him pause, some ten days later, when passing by an estate agent's office as he took his Sunday morning stroll along streets too busy to be pleasant on weekdays – 'There's an explanation for that. Without an occasional change of routine the mind becomes dulled' – he noticed, glancing through the big plate-glass window which the place boasted, a vacuum-cleaner propped up in solitary state in the middle of the outer office. It took him only a few minutes to work out that the machine had been abandoned by thieves the night before when at the last moment they had found it too cumbersome to take with them. He positively trotted along the empty pavements until he reached home and the telephone. The police, when they rang back to say the office cleaner had left the machine there by mistake on Saturday afternoon, were distinctly frosty, almost sub-zero.

But Mr Shelbrake was not deterred. After all, he reasoned, when there was an explanation for something that plainly indicated some crime or another was about to take place or had just been perpetrated, then plainly it was his duty to pass the explanation on. And, once you began to look about you, he told E.L. Ridge one day as they discussed the shortcomings of the jobbing gardener who divided his time between their two properties, it is astonishing how much evidence there is of crimes just past and crimes about to come.

Before long it seemed he had occasion to ring the police as often as once a week, sometimes twice. Or even three times. And eventually he was asked by a senior officer, with rigid politeness, to cease making such calls.

'Of course,' he said to E.L. Ridge when once again he had occasion to bewail the tendency of the gardener to spend more time on E.L. Ridge's side of their dividing wall than on his, even if he did little work wherever he was, 'there's an explanation for that attitude on the part of the police. They are notoriously under-staffed. So, frequently they have to make an arbitary decision simply not to investigate something. And the cases they do choose to tackle are, it follows, those likely to present least difficulty.'

'Oh, no,' E.L. Ridge answered, in his most provoking manner, 'the cases they concentrate on are the ones where they believe they will be bound to fail.'

'Bound to fail? What do you mean?'

The note of bickering had begun to sound, a faint, windblown tocsin.

'What I mean is that human beings, and even our noble police force comes under that category, really wish not to know the reasons for events. Man loves a mystery. And woman, as you know, loves one even more. So, without making any conscious decision, a detective will always devote his best attentions to any puzzle to which he surmises no solution will ever be found.'

'Poppycock.'

The argument – their exchange could be said to have heated up to such a point – lasted all the rest of the evening, branching off as is the way of these things into subjects only remotely connected with the starting-point. Mr Shelbrake had occasion to put forward his explanation of the origin of the word 'cocktail'. It was, he had explained, derived from 'a cock-tailed horse', that is one of mixed or dubious origin as opposed to a sleek-tailed thoroughbred.

'Utter nonsense,' E.L. Ridge had snapped. 'The word just came into somebody's head one day, some bartender somewhere in America, and it caught on.'

'Excuse me, but you're being plainly ridiculous. Nothing, not even a word like cocktail, comes into being without some explanation. Some good, logical explanation.'

And then they had got on to biorhythms, which Mr Shelbrake believed were the explanation underlying almost all the otherwise unexplained oddities of human behaviour.

'And you mean to tell me,' E.L. Ridge had said, had almost snarled, 'that what any one human being does at any one time is controlled by some sort of rhythms set up at his or her birth? I have never heard such appalling claptrap.'

76

'I did not,' Mr Shelbrake had answered, straining not to clench his fists, 'offer an explanation dependent on the mere hour of birth. I stated that behaviour is conditioned by rhythms commencing at the moment of conception. And I challenge you to prove otherwise. Yes, I challenge you.'

Afterwards, lying in bed in his comfortable house next door waiting for sleep to come, Mr Shelbrake decided that, despite the peeps of acrimony that had risen up – he could not remember whether E.L. Ridge had or had not accepted that challenge – their confrontation had on the whole been thoroughly enjoyable. And, he reflected, as his mind dreamily slowed, there is an explanation for that . . . But what it was he did not succeed in formulating.

The days went past. Mr Shelbrake continued to notice evidence of crimes committed or contemplated in the neighbourhood, and he wrote an account of the Charles Bravo murder. It explained, conclusively he claimed, how the death of that five-months married young London lawyer had been at the hands of neither his wife nor his housekeeper nor his wife's former lover but the result only of an accident. Mr Shelbrake was no addict hooked on murder for murder's sake. For him, always, the explanation was the thing.

He longed, almost painfully, to be able as well to report the various explanations for what he had observed in the criminal line in his own quiet neighbourhood. But, after one abortive attempt to go over the head of the local police to Scotland Yard itself, he recognised that circumstances had brought him to a complete check in that direction.

'But you wait,' he said to E.L. Ridge one afternoon

when he had dropped in to discuss the latest peccadillo of their gardener, 'sooner or later there will be a burglary somewhere round about here, possibly with some poor householder badly injured, or even dead, and I will have proof – I shall send it personally to the Minister at the Home Office – that I could have warned them it was going to happen. I make a note of every instance now, you know, signed and dated.'

'And you realise what they will do, even at the Home Office, when you send them your famous memorandum,' E.L. Ridge retorted. 'They'll ignore it, my boy. Simply ignore it.'

'How can you say that? They wouldn't dare. Sooner or later an explanation would be demanded. I would write to my Member of Parliament.'

'But no-one would want an explanation, you know. They'd want it to remain a mystery. A dark and undiscovered mystery.'

And on that occasion – afterwards Mr Shelbrake had been glad of it – the element of heatedness had luckily been dissipated. For some reason or other they had fallen into talking of a less contentious matter, the vagaries of the postman's time of delivery for which Mr Shelbrake had offered a detailed and comprehensive explanation and E.L. Ridge had done no more than counter with a mild suggestion that the fellow was simply a little absent-minded.

Mr Shelbrake was glad that he and his neighbour had parted on amicable terms because that was, as it happened, the last time they ever spoke. A few days later an intruder broke into the house next door and, in the course apparently of stealing E.L. Ridge's fine collection of mysteriosa, battered him to death.

But, weighing with Mr Shelbrake, even more deeply was the fact that he, and he alone, possessed the explanation for the dreadful event. As, in the immediate aftermath, details of the crime percolated round the neighbourhood it had become clear that the murder could have taken place at any time over quite a long period. E.L. Ridge had been even more of a recluse than Mr Shelbrake himself. His whole life had been dedicated to his books – *Mysteries of High Peaks and Lost Plateaux* was lying in manuscript on his desk ready to be sent to his publisher – as well as to enlarging and conserving that collection of mysteriosa. He never had visitors. No daily cleaner came in to threaten the more delicate objects in the collection. He dusted, mostly by vigorous blowing, and swept, a little, himself. He cooked with his own hands the simple meals that hardly kept him from his desk. The garden was left to the jobbing gardener, but that unsatisfactory fellow received only a single mug of tea at each visit, handed to him at the french windows, the very place where the felonious entry had been effected.

Yet, Mr Shelbrake thought, how could he tell the police that in the afternoon of the day before the discovery of the body – the postman had rung E.L. Ridge's doorbell with a set of proofs too bulky to put through the letter-box – he had noticed at the other end of the same passageway where he had seen that battered van many months before the same vehicle waiting? And that it had, again, had its back doors ready open? And that the very same rough-looking driver had been crouched at its wheel?

The explanation of it all was obvious. Frustrated for some reason at their last attempt at robbery, the gang to which the unprepossessing driver belonged had at last got wind of the fact that E.L. Ridge kept in the house, in which he was the sole harmless inhabitant, a collection of highly valuable objects. It would have been, of course, the gardener who had tipped them off. That must be it. The fellow was probably not directly connected to the gang but had been talking loosely in the pub or somewhere. It was all hung together beautifully. The complete explanation. But how could he convince the police?

An officer had actually called shortly after the body had been discovered to ask him if he had seen anybody suspicious loitering nearby. But that had been, in fact, no more important a figure than the man on the local beat. And, when he had begun to give him the outline of the explanation for the affair, he had at once stiffened and said 'Just whether you saw anyone in the immediate vicinity of number thirty-one, sir. If you please.'

'No,' he had said, brushing the inquiry aside. 'No, I did not. But as I was saying—'

'Thank you, sir. You've been most helpful. I'll bid you good morning.'

Later he had tried presenting himself at the local police station and had asked to see whoever was in charge of the investigation into the E.L. Ridge murder. But the sergeant at the desk – he was about half Mr Shelbrake's age – only gave him a fatherly look and said that he didn't think they needed any assistance over what was, after all, a straightforward case.

'But the van, I saw a van—'

'Yes, sir. You told us all about that van. Quite a few months ago it was. We cleared the matter up, if you remember.'

At that Mr Shelbrake turned away, went sadly back to

his house and firmly shut the front door behind him.

There's an explanation for attitudes of that sort, he said to himself wearily. I suppose you could call it the Wolf-wolf Complex.

But he felt too tired to elaborate, even in his own head generally so receptive to the explanations he hit upon.

Yet he found he could not let the matter rest. There must be somebody who would hear his explanation and believe it. But then he remembered all the people who had not believed in his explanations for the Wallace case, the Lizzie Borden affair, the Mrs Maybrick mystery. His last paper, *How Charles Bravo Really Died*, had not even secured a home in print. Perhaps, after all, E.L. Ridge had been right. People did not want explanations: they wanted mysteries, ever unsolved mysteries.

But that thought revolted him.

He took then to staring for hours out of the window of his spare bedroom – he had never had a guest in it – because from there he had a good view of the side-door to E.L. Ridge's house and he could monitor the comings and goings of the police. But, after a day or two more, even these became very infrequent. No doubt, he thought, the murder was now seen as being well on the way to being cleared up. The police would have fixed on some local villain – wasn't that what they called them? Villains – and were simply putting together some sort of case against him. A case without any real, coherent, methodical explanation.

He had worked out who the officer heading the inquiry must be, a tall, slightly hunched hatless figure in a drab belted mackintosh. The explanation of that was obvious: he was the right age to be senior enough to be in charge, he appeared only seldom and he did not, unlike the others going into and coming out of the house, carry anything. He must be, he reckoned, a Detective Inspector. Perhaps a Detective Chief Inspector though, if what the desk sergeant at the station had said about the case being a straightforward matter was right, the inquiry probably didn't merit the attentions of anyone that high in rank.

He stood there at the window, looking down at the fellow's small bald patch and the scanty greying hair – it was just a little curly – surrounding it. He wanted with a fierce longing to know more about the man than this bare physical appearance. What was he actually like? Was he a dyed-in-the-wool follower of routine, incapable of doing anything else but going through the motions with each case that confronted him? Or was he by some wonderful chance a man who could see more than was under his nose? A man who, given an explanation for something a little unexpected, would nevertheless look at it with an unjaundiced eye? Be ready in the end to accept it?

And after all, Mr Shelbrake said to himself, murmuring almost aloud, the explanation of the break-in at E.L. Ridge's house was not particularly out of the way. Stationing a getaway vehicle at one end of a passageway or pedestrian overbridge to foil pursuit by a following car was a well-known criminals' trick. He himself must have read of it half a dozen times in the evening paper.

And what was the Inspector's, or Chief Inspector's, name? Mr Shelbrake began to feel that if he knew that he would somehow have begun to get a handle to his personality. But he knew he could not even go to the police station again and ask that simple question. The desk sergeant had treated him as if he was a lunatic, one of those quiet but persistent madmen who gave the police a lot of trouble, even if it was easily enough dealt with. No, he would be greeted with a look of weary resignation the moment he had got through the outer door.

But then, to his incredulous delight, just two days later, he saw from his high window that bald patch above the stooped shoulders in the drab mackintosh come out of E.L. Ridge's house by the front door, go down the tiled path to the front gate, turn in the direction of his own house and begin walking slowly and, surely, thoughtfully along the pavement towards his own front gate. He had scuttered away from the side-window then and run into his own bedroom where the windows looked directly out on to the road. And yes, yes, the Chief Inspector, or perhaps Inspector, was pushing open his own gate – he heard the familiar squeak of its hinges as if it was a band of high-sounding trumpets – and advancing down his tiled path.

There came a ring at the doorbell. Shaking with excitement, mouth dry, Mr Shelbrake went tumbling down the stairs, ran across to the front door, tugged it open.

'Mr Shelbrake? Detective Superintendent Boothby. Might I have a word?'

His heart leapt up. Now, now at last, the explanation was going to be listened to. And by an officer even higher in rank than a Detective Chief Inspector. Surely a man capable of stepping aside from the pedantic and obvious.

Eagerly he led him into his sitting-room.

'Sit down, sit down, please. I suppose you gathered from the sergeant I spoke to at the station that I have some information – an explanation indeed – that will be of use to you?'

'Yes,' Superintendent Boothby answered. 'I have indeed heard about you. And I have one or two questions I would like to ask.'

'Well, yes, I dare say. But I think you had better hear my explanation of the case first.'

'Something about a van, would that be?'

'Yes, yes. I see you've got on to it already. Excellent. Now, let me tell you the whole thing from the beginning. You see—'

'One moment, sir. I think this may be going to take some time. It might be better if you were to come down to the station.'

Mr Shelbrake suppressed a tiny flicker of irritation. After all, he thought, that probably would be the best course. Explanations, even the simplest of them, do have a way of developing ramifications. They often, alas, take a considerable time to be made fully explicit. Perhaps, indeed, the length of my explanations of things to poor old E.L. Ridge were what caused him at times to become so—well, not to speak too ill of the dead, so cantankerous.

Some seven hours later Mr Shelbrake finished initialling each page of his long statement, which included, among a good deal of other things only marginally relevant, the fact that over the years E.L. Ridge's insistence that everything in life was essentially a mystery had more and more caused friction between them. 'Well, I suppose I should go so far as to say more than friction. Bad blood, to speak the truth. Yes, bad blood.'

Only then had he got on to details of the business of the waiting van, the narrow passageway and the rough-looking driver.

'I had thought at first,' he had said, glancing at the policewoman with the clicking dictation machine to make sure she was still keeping up, 'of putting forward the explanation that it was the jobbing gardener we shared who was responsible for poor Ridge's death. It seemed, on the face of it, the most likely explanation. After all, the fellow is a thoroughly bad lot, no doubt about it.'

'You decided against the postman?' Superintendent Boothby had asked, his patience apparently inexhaustible.

'The postman?'

'Yes, you know that old story-book chestnut? The man nobody's supposed to notice?'

'Oh,' Mr Shelbrake had said, crestfallen. 'I never thought of him.'

A considerable pause in his dictation had followed.

At last he resumed.

'No,' he said. 'The postman was not really necessary. You see, I was really sure, Superintendent, that in the end you would realise that it can only have been myself, his next-door neighbour, who had dealt with that insufferable fellow, Ridge. I'm delighted that you did, you know. Truly delighted. You see, it proves absolutely that in the end always there's an explanation for everything.'

The Lavender Garter

Roger Longrigg

The Lavender Garter

NOVEMBER WAS A BAD MONTH for a hanging. A brown fog clung to the sweating granite of the prison, and seeped between the bars of the cells; it muffled the footfalls in the exercise yard, and the clank of the keys at the warders' belts. The scaffold was clammy in the damp air, its step and trapdoor slippery, the rope as cold and wet as a hawser at the bottom of the sea. Everybody was depressed.

It was not even a glamorous execution, not an actress who had poisoned her lover, or an aristocrat who had stabbed a cheat at the card-table. The newspapers were not interested – no reporters from faraway London were drinking whisky in the taprooms of the town, or paying the turnkeys for interviews. The condemned man was obscure, his trial and conviction almost unreported. Warders, prisoners and all felt cheated by the drabness of the business. The time of year made it worse. A midsummer hanging was cheerful. There had been an almost festive execution in the prison at the beginning of June, a few days after the King's victory in the never-to-be-forgotten Derby – that summer of 1909 was one to savour! But now the fog lay over the countryside like a blanket over a corpse, and the hangman coughed and blew on his hands, and wished the clocks would hurry.

The Acting Chaplain sat in front of a small coal fire, waiting for a summons from the warder. He was a pink and plump young man, only recently ordained, curate of a parish in the town; he had been glad of the extra stipend, for preaching at petty criminals in their cells when the Chaplain was on holiday, but now he was filled with discomfort and dismay. He did not want to sit up all night with a condemned murderer, and go with him in the dawn to the place appointed, and give comfort and guidance, and hear hysterical contrition, and be wept at. If he had foreseen this sort of thing, especially in November, he would never have taken the job.

The parsimonious fire belched yellow smoke, but gave off little heat. The Acting Chaplain felt a cold coming on. He wanted his bed, and a hot whisky toddy.

The warder knocked, and came into the Chaplain's room.

'When you're ready, sir. The prisoner Trenchard is asking for you.'

'Very well.'

The Acting Chaplain followed the warder by labyrinthine granite tunnels, hellishly half-lit by infrequent flares of gas, infiltrated by the clammy fingers of the fog. They passed through the block occupied by the men awaiting trial, remanded in custody, some of whom might in the end, to the fury of the authorities, be found not guilty by their juries: through the wing of the short-term prisoners, professionals doing their two or three months, many among them well known to the staff, almost members of the family, glad to have a roof over their heads for Christmas: then to the grimmer halls of the long sentences, where hope abandoned hung like a miasma between the gas-lamps: and then at last to the terrible ultimate, the end of the last passage, the end of life, the condemned cell.

'He won't give you no trouble, sir,' said the warder. 'It's a weakly, sickly kind of specimen, not like the murderers when I were a lad. If so be as he threatens, a shout will bring me.'

The key was turned in the lock, and the bolts pulled back. The metallic crashes reverberated in that silent place like the shock of iron-clad regiments colliding in battle. The warder ushered the Acting Chaplain into the cell. The door clanged shut. The noise of lock and bolts was even louder.

The prisoner was a scrawny man, rather above the average height, aged about forty, with a thin ginger beard and thin hair. He had an air at once moth-eaten and dogged, the look of a man not resigned to his failure. This was evidently not something acquired in the months of custody, but brought with him. He was already resentful when arrested; here was, perhaps, the reason for his crime. The Acting Chaplain's heart sank when he thought how soon he would hear all about it.

'Ah – Trenchard?'

'You're not the fellow I've been seeing,' said the

prisoner in a sharp, nasal voice. He spoke like a man of education. This would make his story longer.

'The Chaplain is suffering from the grippe. I am his unworthy substitute.'

'You are welcome to my parlour, Reverend Sir, ha ha! We who are about to die salute thee, ha ha!'

'Oh my son, reflect if this is a meet time for bitterness and scorn.'

'For bitterness, yes! Hear my story, and judge. I tell you that I am deserving of my country's honour, my sovereign's recognition. He whom you see doomed and humiliated should be the ornament of chivalry, the toast of salons, the cynosure of all eyes, a reproach to cowardice, an example to youth!'

In spite of his air of hangdog defiance, the prisoner wore his convict's uniform with a certain dandyish swagger, an angry vanity which became more marked as he spoke and gestured.

The Acting Chaplain settled himself, in a listening attitude, on the edge of the prisoner's cot.

'You know, of course,' the condemned man began, 'something of my history. You know my reputation. You have often heard, perhaps sometimes mentioned, the name of Alaric Trenchard.'

'Ahem. That is to say.'

'My God. I have heard of other-worldly clergy in remote provincial places, but I had not suspected a benightedness so inspissate. I am – I was – an artist, not unknown in the galleries of Cork Street and Pall Mall, not unsung in the columns of the critics. I studied in Paris in the nineties. I had coffee once with Claude Monet . . . at least, we were in the same café. On my return to London, I challenged Sickert in Chelsea,

Beardsley in Pimlico. I did not deign to paint for the public, as did they and their toadies. Art for me was the pure spring at which it was privilege enough to drink. I did not seek to sell. I exhibited, though to a large extent excluded from the major galleries by jealousy. So for a dozen years, surviving by dint of a modest legacy from a departed aunt. I did not feast, but I did not starve. I did not despair, but I did not sell. I was the victim of professional small-mindedness and public ignorance. Rembrandt, you know, latterly had the same trouble . . .

'Then Olivia came into my life. It was eighteen months ago – the April of 1908 – in the studio of a sad hack named Cyril Bliss. Someone had brought her to his *vernissage*, he having by some extraordinary vagary been accorded a one-man show at the Cockburn Gallery. I say that Olivia came into my life. I should say rather that she invaded it – exploded into it – took it by storm. Ah, Gods, what a creature! Divinely tall, made after the manner of the nymphs of Arcady, slender, yet abundantly curved, a dimple to her elbow and a waterfall wave to her hair, something Pre-Raphaelite about the set of her chin (I would not have you think that I followed those posturing clowns), something of Titian about that remote and tender smile . . . She was an artist's model. She had posed for fellows who drew for the illustrated papers, and also at life-classes for students of the Slade.'

'Life-classes! You mean – you are suggesting – the lady posed in the – without so much as a—?'

'At once I offered her my protection. We left Cyril Bliss's studio together, dined in Greek Street, I remember, at the little Cent-Neuf hard by Soho Square, and returned at last to my studio in Tite Street. There for twelve months she stayed, bringing such a lamp of golden light to my eyrie, being withal so gracious and bantering a hostess to my visitors, suffering me to paint her hour after hour, day after day, canvas after resplendent canvas – I tell you, she was my muse, my inspiration, my guiding light! And at last I did her justice. I had posed her on a dais half reclining, on the skin of an animal. There was a marvellous contrast between the barbaric texture of the fur and the alabaster purity of my Olivia's skin, especially, perhaps, that of her thighs . . . She wore, as a kind of device, this.'

Alaric Trenchard produced from his pocket a circlet of ruched mauve material, which turned out to be silk gathered about a band of elastic. The Acting Chaplain had never seen such a thing, but he knew that its function was to sustain a female stocking, and that it was called a garter.

'She wore,' he faltered, 'only that?'

'I thought it droll, striking, not without allegory . . . At any rate, the picture was completed in January, and shown at the Spring Exhibition at the Cockburn in March. It was originally entitled *Olivia Girt for Battle*, but in the catalogue they called it *The Lavender Garter*. It was the star of the show, the talk of London. The town was at my feet! My studio was besieged. Gods, what weeks were those! The object itself – this trumpery wisp of fabric – is all that remains to me of that triumph, that peak of my career, that sunlit summit of my life. It was returned to me today, by the kindness of the Chief Warder, from among my effects.

'Olivia left me, for Cyril Bliss. Unknown to me, she had been seeing him for months. With her went my light, my inspiration. Without her, I was destroyed.

Other models were useless to me. *Nature morte* was dead indeed. Landscape was a desert. I tried to paint Olivia from sketches and from memory, but I could not recapture the sheen of her skin, the pink and gold, the dimpled luxury of her . . .'

'In my misery I craved company, distraction. I sought the crowded room, the brilliant lights, the flowing bowl. I went, in a word, to the Café Royal. I am telling you this so that you will understand how I, a man of peace, became involved in matters of life and death. Picture me, then, in the Domino Room, in that magnificence of gilt and of scarlet velvet, great mirrors so placed as to multiply the vista in all directions, clouds of smoke from hundreds of cigars, the hum and babble of intellectual converse, the clattering of dominoes on the marble tables, I forlorn and alone in that fervid Bohemia, desolate and silent, consoling myself with the *sorcière glauque*—'

'The what?'

'The glaucous sorceress, though that does not sound as well. I refer, unfortunately, to absinthe. It goes green when you add water. I madly watched the sinful drip, and madly quaffed the spirit . . . My only companion was this single souvenir of my Olivia, to which I addressed despairing speeches, cursing the treacherous and detestable Cyril Bliss . . . I was requested by the management to leave, and went out into Regent Street. I took the wrong hat. Anybody might have done so, under those circumstances – a broken heart, *la sorcière* . . . It is the single thing that I did wrong, and, under those circumstances, not so great a crime, I think?'

'Please continue,' said the Acting Chaplain.

'I put on the hat of a stranger, and was immediately seized. An arm enfolded me. Two men, three. I was bundled willy-nilly into a cab. I tried to protest, to resist, but no words came, and there was no strength in my limbs. The sorceress had stolen all my powers of speech and movement. But I was treated by those persons not as a victim, nor yet an enemy, but with honour. For a time I thought they knew me. But they addressed me as O'Kelly. What was I to make of that?'

'It was a case of mistaken identity,' suggested the Acting Chaplain.

'Of course it was, Reverend Fool. And so I told them, and they laughed, as though at an excellent jest. Evidently I resembled O'Kelly, but more particularly I had his hat. It was a distinctive hat, velours, primrose-yellow, by which they had been told to know him. It was strange that I should have supposed such a dreadful hat to be mine. These are the ways of absinthe; you see, therefore, that Octavia and Cyril Bliss are to be blamed for my predicament. The cab arrived at long last in a remote and squalid quarter of London, a warren of courts and alleys into which, I dare swear, neither the sun nor the Metropolitan Police had ever penetrated. I was put, I suppose, to bed. I awoke with a headache. I was conducted into a closely shuttered room.

' "Good morning, Comrade!" cried a giant of a man with a great black beard, a hooked nose, a jutting brow. He introduced himself as Vladimir, in a manner that showed that he assumed I knew who he was, and all about him.

' "There has been a dreadful mistake," I stammered. "My name is Trenchard."

'Vladimir laughed, a noise like thunder. "Very good! Excellent! Of course you go in London by a *nom de guerre*."

'My headache had intensified. I had not strength enough to convince him of the truth. I allowed myself to be O'Kelly. As O'Kelly I was presented to the three silent men with Balkan names who had kidnapped me in Regent Street, and to a lady called Dagmar. She was of startling beauty – raven-haired, statuesque, with eyes of such fanatic brilliance that I felt them burning into my soul. I was frightened of the giant Vladimir, but I was more frightened of Dagmar.

'They asked me about the progress of affairs in America. I told them I knew nothing of America. They laughed, and applauded my caution. They said that I was a hero, a martyr, that my name would ring down history for my part in the great event. What event? They laughed. They thought I knew, that I had come from America especially to take part in – what?

'Gradually I realised what they were talking about. Who they were. What they planned. My blood froze. My headache became worse.

'They were anarchists. They were going to detonate an enormous bomb. I was to help. I was to give my life in the explosion. I had volunteered to do so. Dagmar also. She and I were to die together, to go up gloriously for the cause.

' "By this act of magnificent destruction," cried Dagmar, "We shall strike a blow at the very heart of this corrupt and decadent so-called civilisation, where self-indulgent greed tramples the faces of the starving, who are too weak and ignorant to fight their oppressor."

'I was all too familiar with this line of talk, which I used to hear at great length in Paris. I never thought to be in the midst of a serious gang of such, nor that the windy rhetoric of the Left Bank cafés would solidify into a great sack of dynamite!

'I noticed now that they all had pistols. Dagmar, indeed, had two small pistols, Vladimir only one, but that a cannon. I realised that I was in a position of extreme danger. They thought that I was one of them, committed to their cause, prepared to give my life. Thus they spoke freely, talking of all their plans, making me privy to all their secrets. If they now suspected that I was not O'Kelly – I would be dead within seconds. My body would be found, perhaps, in the Thames, with a knife in the heart . . .

'I no longer protested that I was Alaric Trenchard, artist, wearer by mischance of a stranger's hat.

'Casually I searched through my pockets for anything that might be of use, anything that might serve as a weapon. I had no cigar-cutter, penknife, letter-opener; not so much as a pencil. I had Olivia's lavender garter: that was all.

'Three days and nights I lived with them in that den, desperate to sustain the deception, alert every second for a chance to escape. None came. Meanwhile I learned, with mounting horror, what they planned. The place of the explosion was to be the grandstand of Epsom Races, and the time was to be the moment of the finish of the Derby. Oh, imagine it! A gigantic concourse of people, the flower of the aristocracy, His Majesty and all the royal family – all eyes on the racecourse – plenty of noise and excitement to cover the foul deed, and to permit the escape of all save Dagmar and myself. We, of course, were to be at the very centre of the explosion, for ours was the task of detonating the dynamite. Dagmar's eyes blazed when she spoke of it. Martyrdom was sweet to her.

'In the dark before the dawn of Wednesday the twenty-sixth of May, we climbed into a large closed carriage – Vladimir, the other three, Dagmar and myself, having loaded three wooden crates and a suitcase onto the roof, for we were carrying with us the explosive and the electrical equipment for detonating it. It was worrying to trundle over the uneven streets with three crates of dynamite a foot above one's head. The others laughed about it.

'We made good time, the roads being still empty, and it was hardly sunrise when the carriage drew up behind the grandstand. Vladimir had made his preparations well – one policeman passed us to another, he to a functionary of the grandstand. Vladimir's bribery had secured documents and passes. The dynamite was masquerading as champagne. Thus it was welcomed into the very heart of the grandstand!

'As the light strengthened, I was able to see that Vladimir and the others were dressed as waiters. "We can go anywhere, at any time, unquestioned," said Vladimir, with a laugh that froze my blood.

'It was at this point that Dagmar gave me one of her pistols. "Use it if you must," she said, "to protect our mission. If you kill a man before the explosion, you will but advance his death by a few seconds."

'She showed me how to load, cock and fire the weapon. For a moment I considered shooting them all, there and then. But it was impossible. I had to bide my time, and hope.

'There was such a bustle in the grandstand in the dawn, such a crowd of cooks and scullions preparing such a quantity of food, that it was easy to go anywhere, as Vladimir said. So many cases of wine and crates of glasses, so many baskets of plates and hampers of food were being carried up and down stairs, that our boxes were quite unnoticed. If challenged, we were to say that we were serving a private party. Thus the dynamite could be unpacked and hidden about the grandstand almost without effort of concealment, and the wires to the detonator laid as though by innocent artisans.

'One had to admire the fiendish ingenuity of it – not only was this the most shockingly murderous of all possible explosions, with the densest crowd of the greatest people of the entire year – not only would it cause the most extraordinary sensation throughout the world, but it was the simplest and safest to prepare.

'Long before the public began to arrive, Vladimir's preparations were complete.

'The dynamite was strategically deployed in a dozen places where it would most utterly demolish the structure of the enormous grandstand. The effect would thus be doubled – while the explosions would kill half the crowd, falling masonry would kill the rest. All the bundles of dynamite were wired to a single detonator, which would set them all off at the same moment. It was this arrangement which called for the martyrdom of Dagmar and myself. It was even, perhaps, her plan.

'The day promised to be the fairest of the summer. From the heights of the grandstand, we could see, Dagmar and I, the whole world gradually converging on Epsom Downs – the gypsies and their caravans, the showmen and their booths, the publicans and their tents and barrels – horses, carts, omnibuses, automobiles, uncounted armies were advancing onto the Downs, bespangling with brilliant colour the great pale sweep of the hill. Into the grandstand, too, the flood began, silk dresses, parasols, tall hats, happy shouts, excitement, music from below, from half a dozen bands, the murmur of waiters, the pop of corks, flirtations, bold girls, bashful boys . . . Oh, Parson, I was to be party to the wholesale slaughter of them all!'

The condemned man plucked at his scanty beard. His hand shook. Recollection of that terrible day was almost too much for him.

The Acting Chaplain was quite interested to know what happened next.

'I was too distraught to follow the events of the day,' Alaric Trenchard went on, 'the running of the earlier races, all the celebrations and excitements. I clearly remember only the extraordinary sense of festivity, as though this were the greatest and most jocund of all national holidays. You understand how awful was that irony.

'The hour of the great race approached. The horses paraded in the paddock, distant specks from our vantage-point. The crowd was ever thicker, more excited, noisier. I fingered the pistol in my pocket, and suddenly knew my duty. I was appalled. Regardless of the consequences to myself, regardless of my feelings, my conscience even, I must shoot Dagmar down like a dog, just before she thrust down the plunger of the detonator.

'I was sick with horror and suspense: the worse because all about was an ever-mounting maelstrom of merriment. And the sun shone and the girls were so pretty!

'Dimly I was aware that the horses were leaving the paddock – were going out through the crowds, and on to the Downs, and up the hill to the start. All the world was looking at those distant specks – but I had eyes only for Dagmar, who under cover of a shawl was gripping the plunger of the detonator.

'There about us was the largest crowd ever assembled, even for the Derby. There below us were the King and court, a large proportion of the aristocracy, of Parliament, of Bench and Bar, the most senior officers of the army and navy, the luminaries of art and literature, the ornaments of the stage . . .

' "They're off!" was called by a million throats, and there was throughout the gigantic crowd a mounting murmur of excitement, which grew in volume and depth and shrillness, as the horses came to the top of the hill, and started down towards Tattenham Corner – and Dagmar shrugged aside the shawl, so that I saw her fingers tighten on the detonator's handgrip, her knuckles whitening, her eyes burning with fanatic zeal . . .

'In the storm of noise, I drew out Dagmar's own small pistol, aimed at her heart, and fired!'

'Heaven preserve us!' cried the Acting Chaplain.

'Heaven preserved Dagmar,' said the condemned man. 'Have you ever tried, when in a state of extreme tension, to hit so small a target as a person, at a range of six feet, with a lady's pistol?'

'Never,' declared the Acting Chaplain.

'It is exceedingly difficult. I missed. I fired three times, the noise of the gun almost inaudible in the general din, taken no doubt if heard as the pop of corks coming out of bottles. Dagmar herself heard nothing. She was unaware of being fired at. The bullets, I suppose, flew harmlessly somewhere out into the void.

'The horses were thundering up towards the winning-post, in a veritable cauldron of noise.

' "Minoru," screamed a million voices.

'A part of my brain registered that the King's horse had won.

'Dagmar's moment had arrived.

'Hardly knowing what I was doing, driven by some sudden instinct to try to distract her, I flicked at her a piece of elastic that found itself in my fingers. The garter! It did distract her, the frivolity at such a moment, the colour. She paused, stumbled, letting go of the detonator in order to grasp the parapet behind which we stood. I took a step towards her, put a hand to her shoulder, pushed. She staggered. She screamed. Nobody heard, because everybody was screaming. She fell over the parapet. She fell to her death two hundred feet below, on the flagstones of a passage leading to the cellars of the grandstand.

'I tore the wires from the detonator. The dynamite was now harmless.'

'I see the hand of Providence,' murmured the Acting Chaplain, awestruck.

'I was able to tell the police where the dynamite was hidden,' said Alaric Trenchard. 'But Vladimir and his friends got clear away.'

'Was not this amazing story told at your trial?'

'No. Not a word of it.'

'But why, in Heaven's name? It is true that you encompassed the death of the woman Dagmar, but she would have killed herself, with a million others, a second later!'

'Oh yes. I was not arrested for her death. When I came away from Epsom, I was anxious to improve my performance with Dagmar's pistol. I practised shooting, using as my target a rust-coloured cotton coat. My

103

marksmanship was better. I hit the very mark I was aiming at, above the left breast of the coat.'

'What of it?' asked the Acting Chaplain, puzzled by this turn of the prisoner's tale.

'Cyril Bliss was wearing the coat.'

The Crime of
Miss Oyster Brown

Peter Lovesey

The Crime of Miss Oyster Brown

MISS OYSTER BROWN, A DEVOUT member of the Church of England, joined passionately each Sunday in every prayer of the Morning Service – except for the general Confession, when, in all honesty, she found it difficult to class herself as a lost sheep. She was willing to believe that everyone else in church had erred and strayed. In certain cases she knew exactly how, and with whom, and she would say a prayer for them. On her own account, however, she could seldom think of anything to confess. She tried strenuously, more strenuously – dare I say it? – than you or me to lead an untainted life. She managed conspicuously well. Very occasionally, as the rest of the congregation joined in the Confession, she would own up to some trifling sin.

You may imagine what a fall from grace it was when

this virtuous woman committed not merely a sin, but a crime. She lived more than half her life before it happened.

She resided in a Berkshire town with her twin sister Pearl, who was a mere three minutes her senior. Oyster and Pearl – a flamboyance in forenames that owed something to the fact that their parents had been plain John and Mary Brown. Up to the moment of birth the Browns had been led to expect one child who, if female, was to be named Pearl. In the turmoil created by a second, unscheduled, daughter, John Brown jokingly suggested naming her Oyster. Mary, bosky from morphine, seized on the name as an inspiration, a delight to the ear when said in front of dreary old Brown. Of course the charm was never so apparent to the twins, who got to dread being introduced to people. Even in infancy they were aware that their parents' friends found the names amusing. At school they were taunted as much by the teachers as the children. The names never ceased to amuse. Fifty years on, things were still said just out of earshot and laced with pretended sympathy. 'Here come Pearl and Oyster, poor old ducks. Fancy being stuck with names like that.'

No wonder they faced the world defiantly. In middle age they were a formidable duo, stalwarts of the choir, the Bible Reading Circle, the Townswomen's Guild and the Magistrates' Bench. Neither sister had married. They lived together in Lime Tree Avenue, in the mock-Tudor house where they were born. They were not short of money.

There are certain things people always want to know about twins, the more so in mystery stories. I can reassure the wary reader that Oyster and Pearl were not identical; Oyster was an inch taller, more sturdy in build than her sister and slower of speech. They dressed individually, Oyster as a rule in tweed skirts and check blouses that she made herself, always from the same Butterick pattern, Pearl in a variety of mail-order suits in pastel blues and greens. No-one confused them. As for that other question so often asked about twins, neither sister could be characterised as 'dominant'. Each possessed a forceful personality by any standard. To avoid disputes they had established a household routine, a division of the duties, that worked pretty harmoniously, all things considered. Oyster did most of the cooking and the gardening, for example, and Pearl attended to the housework and paid the bills when they became due. They both enjoyed shopping, so they shared it. They did the church flowers together when their turn came, and they always ran the bottle stall at the church fête. Five vicars had held the living at St Saviour's in the twins' time as worshippers there. Each new incumbent was advised by his predecessor that Pearl and Oyster were the mainstays of the parish. Better to fall foul of the diocesan bishop himself than the Brown twins.

All of this was observed from a distance, for no-one, not even a vicar making his social rounds, was allowed inside the house in Lime Tree Avenue. The twins didn't entertain, and that was final. They were polite to their neighbours without once inviting them in. When one twin was ill, the other would transport her to the surgery in a state of high fever rather than call the doctor on a visit.

It followed that people's knowledge of Pearl and

Oyster was limited. No-one could doubt that they lived an orderly existence; there were no complaints about undue noise, or unwashed windows or neglected paintwork. The hedge was trimmed and the lawn mown. But what really bubbled and boiled behind the regularly washed net curtains – the secret passion that was to have such a dire result – was unsuspected until Oyster committed her crime.

She acted out of desperation. On the last Saturday in July, 1991, her well-ordered life suffered a seismic shock. She was parted from her twin sister. The parting was sudden, traumatic and had to be shrouded in secrecy. The prospect of anyone finding out what had occurred was unthinkable.

So for the first time in her life Oyster had no Pearl to change the light bulbs, pay the bills and check that all the doors were locked. Oyster – let it be understood – was not incapable or dim-witted. Bereft as she was, she managed tolerably well until the Friday afternoon, when she had a letter to post, a letter of surpassing importance, capable – God willing – of easing her desolation. She had agonised over it for hours. Now it was crucial that the letter caught the last post of the day. Saturday would be too late. She went to the drawer where Pearl always kept the postage stamps and – calamity – not one was left.

Stamps had always been Pearl's responsibility. To be fair, the error was Oyster's; she had written more letters than usual and gone through the supply. She should have called at the Post Office when she was doing the shopping.

It was too late. There wasn't time to get there before the last post at 5.15. She tried to remain calm and consider her options. It was out of the question to ask a neighbour for a stamp; she and Pearl had made it a point of honour never to be beholden to anyone else. Neither could she countenance the disgrace of despatching the letter without a stamp in the hope that it would get by, or the recipient would pay the amount due.

This left one remedy, and it was criminal.

Behind one of the Staffordshire dogs on the mantelpiece was a bank statement. She had put it there for the time being because she had been too busy to check where Pearl normally stored such things. The significant point for Oyster at this minute was not the statement, but the envelope containing it. More precisely, the top right-hand corner of the envelope, because the first class stamp had somehow escaped being cancelled.

Temptation stirred and uncoiled itself.

Oyster had never in her life steamed an unfranked stamp from an envelope and used it again. Nor, to her knowledge, had Pearl. Stamp collectors sometimes removed used specimens for their collections, but what Oyster was contemplating could in no way be confused with philately. It was against the law. Defrauding the Post Office. A crime.

There was under twenty minutes before the last collection.

I couldn't, she told herself. *I'm on the Parochial Church Council. I'm on the Bench.*

Temptation reminded her that she was due for a cup of tea in any case. She filled the kettle and pressed the switch. While waiting, watching the first wisp of steam rise from the spout, she weighed the necessity of posting the letter against the wickedness of re-using a stamp. It was not the most heinous of crimes, Temptation whispered. And once Oyster began to think about the chances of getting away with it, she was lost. The kettle sang, the steam gushed and she snatched up the envelope and jammed it against the spout. Merely, Temptation reassured her, to satisfy her curiosity as to whether stamps could be separated from envelopes by this method.

Those who believe in retribution will not be in the least surprised that the steam was deflected by the surface of the envelope and scalded three of Oyster's fingers quite severely. She cried out in pain and dropped the envelope. She ran the cold tap and plunged her hand under it. Then she wrapped the sore fingers in a piece of kitchen towel.

Her first action after that was to turn off the kettle. Her second was to pick up the envelope and test the corner of the stamp with the tip of her fingernail. It still adhered to some extent, but with extreme care she was able to ease it free, consoled that her discomfort had not been entirely without result. The minor accident failed to deter her from the crime. On the contrary, it acted like a prod from Old Nick.

There was a bottle of gum in the writing desk and she applied some to the back of the stamp, taking care not to use too much, which might have oozed out at the edges and discoloured the envelope. When she had positioned the stamp neatly on her letter, it would have passed the most rigorous inspection. She felt a wicked frisson of satisfaction at having committed an undetectable crime. Just in time, she remembered the post and had to hurry to catch it.

There we leave Miss Oyster Brown to come to terms with her conscience for a couple of days.

We meet her again on the Monday morning in the local chemist's shop. The owner and pharmacist was John Trigger, whom the Brown twins had known for getting on for thirty years, a decent, obliging man with a huge moustache who took a personal interest in his customers. In the face of strong competition from a national chain of pharmacists, John Trigger had persevered with his old-fashioned service from behind a counter, believing that some customers still preferred it to filling a wire basket themselves. But to stay in business he had been forced to diversify by offering some electrical goods.

When Oyster Brown came in and showed him three badly scalded fingers out in blisters, Trigger was sympathetic as well as willing to suggest a remedy. Understandably he enquired how Oyster had come by such a painful injury. She was expecting the question and had her answer ready, adhering to the truth as closely as a God-fearing woman should.

'An accident with the kettle.'

Trigger looked genuinely alarmed. 'An electric kettle? Not the one you bought here last year?'

'I didn't,' said Oyster at once.

'Must have been your sister. A Steamquick. Is that what you've got?'

'Er, yes.'

'If there's a fault . . .'

'I'm not here to complain, Mr Trigger. So you think this ointment will do the trick?'

'I'm sure of it. Apply it evenly, and don't attempt to pierce the blisters, will you?' John Trigger's conscience was troubling him. 'This is quite a nasty scalding, Miss Brown. Where exactly did the steam come from?'

'The kettle.'

'I know that. I mean was it the spout?'

'It really doesn't matter,' said Oyster sharply. 'It's done.'

'The lid, then? Sometimes if you're holding the handle you get a rush of steam from that little slot in the lid. I expect it was that.'

'I couldn't say,' Oyster fudged, in the hope that it would satisfy Mr Trigger.

It did not. 'The reason I asked is that there may be a design fault.'

'The fault was mine. I'm quite sure.'

'Perhaps I ought to mention it to the manufacturers.'

'Absolutely not,' Oyster said in alarm. 'I was careless, that's all. And now, if you'll excuse me . . .' She started backing away and then Mr Trigger ambushed her with another question.

'What does your sister say about it?'

'My sister?' From the way she spoke, she might never have had one.

'Miss Pearl.'

'Oh, nothing. We haven't discussed it,' Oyster truthfully stated.

'But she must have noticed your fingers.'

'Er, no. How much is the ointment?'

Trigger told her and she dropped the money on the counter and almost rushed from the shop. He stared after her, bewildered.

The next time Oyster Brown was passing, Trigger took the trouble to go to the door of his shop and enquire whether the hand was any better. Clearly she wasn't overjoyed to see him. She assured him without much gratitude that the ointment was working. 'It was nothing. It's going to clear up in a couple of days.'

'May I see?'

She held out her hand.

Trigger agreed that it was definitely on the mend. 'Keep it dry, if you possibly can. Who does the washing up?'

'What do you mean?'

'You, or your sister? It's well known that you divide the chores between you. If it's your job, I'm sure Miss Pearl won't mind taking over for a few days. If I see her, I'll suggest it myself.'

Oyster reddened and said nothing.

'I was going to remark that I haven't seen her for a week or so,' Trigger went on. 'She isn't unwell, I hope?'

'No,' said Oyster. 'Not unwell.'

Sensing correctly that this was not an avenue of conversation to venture along at this time, he said instead, 'The Steamquick rep was in yesterday afternoon, so I mentioned what happened with your kettle.'

She was outraged. 'You had no business.'

'Pardon me, Miss Brown, but it *is* my business. You were badly scalded. I can't have my customers being injured by the products I sell. The rep was very concerned, as I am. He asked if you would be so good as to bring the kettle in next time you come, so that he can check if there's a fault.'

'Absolutely not,' said Oyster. 'I told you I haven't the slightest intention of complaining.'

Trigger tried to be reasonable. 'It isn't just your kettle. I've sold the same model to other customers.'

'Then they'll complain if they get hurt.'

115

'What if their children get hurt?'

She had no answer.

'If it's inconvenient to bring it in, perhaps I could call at your house.'

'No,' she said at once.

'I can bring a replacement. In fact, Miss Brown, I'm more than a little concerned about this whole episode. I'd like you to have another kettle with my compliments. A different model. Frankly, the modern trend is for jug kettles that couldn't possibly scald you as yours did. If you'll kindly step into the shop, I'll give you one now to take home.'

The offer didn't appeal to Oyster Brown in the least. 'For the last time, Mr Trigger,' she said in a tight, clipped voice, 'I don't require another kettle.' With that, she walked away up the high street.

Trigger, from the motives he had mentioned, was not content to leave the matter there. He wasn't a churchgoer, but he believed in conducting his life on humanitarian principles. On this issue, he was resolved to be just as stubborn as she. He went back into the shop and straight to the phone. While Oyster Brown was out of the house, he would speak to Pearl Brown, the sister, and see if he could get better co-operation from her.

Nobody answered the phone.

At lunchtime, he called in to see Ted Collins, who ran the garden shop next door, and asked if he had seen anything of Pearl Brown lately.

'I had Oyster in this morning,' Collins told him.

'But you haven't seen Pearl?'

'Not in my shop. Oyster does all the gardening, you know. They divide the work.'

'I know.'

'I can't think what came over her today. Do you know what she bought? Six bottles of Rapidrot.'

'What's that?'

'It's a new product. An activator for composting. You dilute it and water your compost heap and it speeds up the process. They're doing a special promotion to launch it. Six bottles are far too much, and I tried to tell her, but she wouldn't be told.'

'Those two often buy in bulk,' said Trigger. 'I've sold Pearl a dozen tubes of toothpaste at a go, and they must be awash with Dettol.'

'They won't use six bottles of Rapidrot in twenty years,' Collins pointed out. 'It's concentrated stuff, and it won't keep all that well. It's sure to solidify after a time. I told her one's plenty to be going on with. She's wasted her money, obstinate old bird. I don't know what Pearl would say. Is she ill, do you think?'

'I've no idea,' said Trigger, although in reality an idea was beginning to form in his brain. A disturbing idea. 'Do they get on all right with each other? Daft question,' he said before Collins could answer it. 'They're twins. They've spent all their lives in each other's company.'

For the present he dismissed the thought and gave his attention to the matter of the electric kettles. He'd already withdrawn the Steamquick kettles from sale. He got on the phone to Steamquick and had an acrimonious conversation with some little Hitler from their public relations department who insisted that thousands of the kettles had been sold and the design was faultless.

'The lady's injury isn't imagined, I can tell you,' Trigger insisted.

'She must have been careless. Anyone can hurt

themselves if they're not careful. People are far too ready to put the blame on the manufacturer.'

'People, as you put it, are your livelihood.'

There was a heavy sigh. 'Send us the offending kettle, and we'll test it.'

'That isn't so simple.'

'Have you offered to replace it?'

The man's whole tone was so condescending that Trigger had an impulse to frighten him rigid. 'She won't let the kettle out of her possession. I think she may be keeping it as evidence.'

'Evidence?' There was a pause while the implication dawned. 'Blimey.'

On his end of the phone, Trigger permitted himself to grin.

'You mean she might take us to court over this?'

'I didn't say that—'

'Ah.'

'—but she does know the law. She's a magistrate.'

An audible gasp followed, then: 'Listen, Mr, er –'

'Trigger.'

'Mr Trigger. I think we'd better send someone to meet this lady and deal with the matter personally. Yes, that's what we'll do.'

Trigger worked late that evening, stocktaking. He left the shop about 10.30. Out of curiosity he took a route home via Lime Tree Avenue and stopped the car opposite the Brown sisters' house and wound down the car window. There were lights upstairs and presently someone drew a curtain. It looked like Oyster Brown.

'Keeping an eye on your customers, Mr Trigger?' a voice close to him said.

He turned guiltily. A woman's face was six inches

118

from his. He recognised one of his customers, Mrs Wingate. She said, 'She's done that every night this week.'

'Oh?'

'Something fishy's going on in there,' she said. 'I walk my little dog along the verge about this time every night. I live just opposite them, on this side, with the wrought iron gates. That's Pearl's bedroom at the front. I haven't seen Pearl for a week, but every night her sister Oyster draws the curtains and leaves the light on for half an hour. What's going on, I'd like to know? If Pearl is ill, they ought to call a doctor. They won't, you know.'

'That's Pearl's bedroom, you say, with the light on?'

'Yes, I often see her looking out. Not lately.'

'And now Oyster switches on the light and draws the curtains?'

'And pulls them back at seven in the morning. I don't know what you think, Mr Trigger, but it looks to me as if she wants everyone to think Pearl's in there, when it's obvious she isn't.'

'Why is it obvious?'

'All the windows are closed. Pearl always opens the top window wide, winter and summer.'

'That is odd, now you mention it.'

'I'll tell you one thing,' said Mrs Wingate, regardless that she had told him several things already. 'Whatever game she's up to, we won't find out. Nobody ever sets foot inside the house except the twins themselves.'

At home and in bed that night, Trigger was troubled by a gruesome idea, one that he'd tried repeatedly to suppress. Suppose the worst had happened a week ago in the house in Lime Tree Avenue, his thinking ran.

Suppose Pearl Brown had suffered a heart attack and died. After so many years of living in that house as if it were a fortress, was Oyster capable of dealing with the aftermath of death, calling in the doctor and the undertaker? In her shocked state, mightn't she decide that anything was preferable to having the house invaded, even if the alternative was disposing of the body herself?

How would a middle-aged woman dispose of a body? Oyster didn't drive a car. It wouldn't be easy to bury it in the garden, nor hygienic to keep it in a cupboard in the house. But if there was one thing every well-bred English lady knew about, it was gardening. Oyster was the gardener.

In time, everything rots in a compost heap. If you want to accelerate the process, you buy a preparation like Rapidrot.

Oyster Brown had purchased six bottles of the stuff. And every night she drew the curtains in her sister's bedroom to give the impression that she was there.

He shuddered.

In the fresh light of morning, John Trigger told himself that his morbid imaginings couldn't be true. They were the delusions of a tired brain. He decided to do nothing about them.

Just after 11.30, a short, fat man in a dark suit arrived in the shop and announced himself as the Area Manager of Steamquick. His voice was suspiciously like the one that Trigger had found so irritating when he had phoned their head office. 'I'm here about this allegedly faulty kettle,' he announced.

'Miss Brown's?'

'I'm sure there's nothing wrong at all, but we're a responsible firm. We take every complaint seriously.'

'You want to see the kettle? You'll be lucky.'

The Steamquick man sounded smug. 'That's all right. I telephoned Miss Brown this morning and offered to go to the house. She wasn't at all keen on that idea, but I was very firm with the lady, and she compromised. We're meeting here at noon. She's agreed to bring the kettle for me to inspect. I don't know why you found her so intractable.'

'High noon, eh? Do you want to use my office?'

Trigger had come to a rapid decision. If Oyster was on her way to the shop, he was going out. He had two capable assistants.

This was a heaven-sent opportunity to lay his macabre theory to rest. While Oyster was away from the house in Lime Tree Avenue, he would drive there and let himself into the back garden. Mrs Wingate or any other curious neighbour watching from behind the lace curtains would have to assume he was trying to deliver something. He kept his white coat on, to reinforce the idea that he was on official business.

Quite probably, he told himself, the compost heap will turn out to be no bigger than a cowpat. The day was sunny and he felt positively cheerful as he turned up the Avenue. He checked his watch. Oyster would be making mincemeat of the Steamquick man about now. It would take her twenty minutes, at least, to walk back.

He stopped the car and got out. Nobody was about, but just in case he was being observed he walked boldly up the path to the front door and rang the bell. No-one came.

Without appearing in the least furtive, he stepped around the side of the house. The back garden was in a beautiful state. Wide, well-stocked and immaculately weeded borders enclosed a finely-trimmed lawn, yellow roses on a trellis and a kitchen garden beyond. Trigger took it in admiringly, and then remembered why he was there. His throat went dry. At the far end, beyond the kitchen garden, slightly obscured by some runner beans on poles, was the compost heap – as long as a coffin and more than twice as high.

The flesh on his arms prickled.

The compost heap was covered with black plastic bin-liners weighted with stones. They lay across the top, but the sides were exposed. A layer of fresh green garden refuse, perhaps half a metre in depth, was on the top. The lower part graduated in colour from a dull yellow to earth-brown. Obvious care had been taken to conserve the shape, to keep the pressure even and assist the composting process.

Trigger wasn't much of a gardener. He didn't have the time for it. He did the minimum and got rid of his garden rubbish with bonfires. Compost heaps were outside his experience, except that as a scientist he understood the principle by which they generated heat in a confined space. Once, years ago, an uncle of his had demonstrated this by pushing a bamboo cane into his heap from the top. A wisp of steam had issued from the hole as he withdrew the cane. Recalling it now, Trigger felt a wave of nausea.

He hadn't the stomach for this.

He knew now that he wasn't going to able to walk up the garden and probe the compost heap. Disgusted with himself for being so squeamish, he turned to leave, and happened to notice that the kitchen window was ajar, which was odd, considering that Oyster was not at home. Out of interest he tried the door handle. The door was unlocked.

He said, 'Anyone there?' and got no answer.

From the doorway he could see a number of unopened letters on the kitchen table. After the humiliation of turning his back on the compost heap, this was like a challenge, a chance to regain some self-respect. This, at least, he was capable of doing. He stepped inside and picked up the letters. There were five, all addressed to Miss P. Brown. The postmarks dated from the beginning of the previous week.

Quite clearly Pearl had not been around to open her letters.

Then his attention was taken by an extraordinary line-up along a shelf. He counted fifteen packets of cornflakes, all open, and recalled his conversation with Ted Collins about the sisters buying in bulk. If Collins had wanted convincing, there was ample evidence here: seven bottles of decaffinated coffee, nine jars of the same brand of marmalade and a tall stack of boxes of paper tissues. Eccentric housekeeping, to say the least. Perhaps, he reflected, it meant that the buying of six bottles of Rapidrot had not, after all, been so sinister.

Now that he was in the house, he wasn't going to leave without seeking an answer to the main mystery, the disappearance of Pearl. His mouth was no longer dry and the gooseflesh had gone from his arms. He made up his mind to go upstairs and look into the front bedroom.

On the other side of the kitchen door more extravagance was revealed. The passage from the kitchen to the stairway was lined on either side with sets of goods that must have overflowed from the kitchen. Numerous tins of cocoa, packets of sugar, pots of jam, gravy powder and other grocery items were stored as if for a siege, stacked along the skirting boards in groups of at least half a dozen. Trigger began seriously to fear for the mental health of the twins. Nobody had suspected anything like this behind the closed doors. The stacks extended halfway upstairs.

As he stepped upwards, obliged to tread close to the banisters, he was gripped by the sense of alienation that must have led to hoarding on such a scale. The staid faces that the sisters presented to the world gave no intimation of this strange compulsion. What was the mentality of people who behaved as weirdly as this?

An appalling possibility crept into Trigger's mind. Maybe the strain of so many years of appearing outwardly normal had finally caused Oyster to snap. What if the eccentricity so apparent all around him were not so harmful as it first appeared? No-one could know what resentments, what jealousies lurked in this house, what mean-minded cruelties the sisters may have inflicted on each other. What if Oyster had fallen out with her sister and attacked her? She was a sturdy woman, physically capable of killing.

If she'd murdered Pearl, the compost-heap method of disposal would certainly commend itself.

Come now, he told himself. This is all speculation.

He reached the top stair and discovered that the stockpiling had extended to the landing. Toothpaste, talcum powder, shampoos and soap were stacked up in profusion. All the doors were closed. It wouldn't have surprised him if when he opened one he was knee deep in toilet rolls.

First he had to orientate himself. He decided that the front bedroom was to his right. He opened it cautiously and stepped in.

What happened next was swift and devastating. John Trigger heard a piercing scream. He had a sense of movement to his left and a glimpse of a figure in white. Something crashed against his head with a mighty thump, causing him to pitch forward.

About four, when the Brown twins generally stopped for tea, Oyster filled the new kettle that the Steamquick Area Manager had exchanged for the other one. She plugged it in. It was the new-fangled jug type, and she wasn't really certain if she was going to like it, but she certainly needed the cup of tea.

'I know it was wrong,' she said, 'and I'm going to pray for forgiveness, but I didn't expect that steaming a stamp off a letter would lead to this. I suppose it's a judgement.'

'Whatever made you do such a wicked thing?' her sister Pearl asked, as she put out the cups and saucers.

'The letter had to catch the post. It was the last possible day for the Kellogg's Cornflakes competition, and I'd thought of such a wonderful slogan. The prize was a fortnight in Venice.'

Pearl clicked her tongue in disapproval. 'Just because I won the Birds Eye trip to the Bahamas, it didn't mean you were going to be lucky. We tried for twenty years and only ever won consolation prizes.'

'It isn't really gambling, is it?' said Oyster. 'It isn't like betting.'

'It's all right in the Lord's eyes,' Pearl told her. 'It's a harmless pastime. Unfortunately we both know that people in the church wouldn't take a charitable view. They wouldn't expect us to devote so much of our time

125

and money to competitions. That's why we have to be careful. You didn't tell anyone I was away?'

'Of course not. Nobody knows. For all they know, you were ill, if anyone noticed at all. I drew the curtains in your bedroom every night to make it look as if you were here.'

'Thank you. You know I'd do the same for you.'

'I might win,' said Oyster. 'Someone always does. I put in fifteen entries altogether, and the last one was a late inspiration.'

'And as a result we have fifteen packets of cornflakes with the tops cut off,' said Pearl. 'They take up a lot of room.'

'So do your frozen peas. I had to throw two packets away to make some room in the freezer. Anyway, I felt entitled to try. It wasn't much fun being here alone, thinking of you sunning yourself in the West Indies. To tell you the truth, I didn't really think you'd go and leave me here. It was a shock.' Oyster carefully poured some hot water into the teapot to warm it. 'If you want to know, I've also entered the Rapidrot Trip of a Lifetime competition. A week in San Francisco followed by a week in Sydney. I bought six bottles to have a fighting chance.'

'What's Rapidrot?'

'Something for the garden.' She spooned in some tea and poured on the hot water. 'You must be exhausted. Did you get any sleep on the plane?'

'Hardly any,' said Pearl. 'That's why I went straight to bed when I got in this morning.' She poured milk into the teacups. 'The next thing I knew was the doorbell going. I ignored it, naturally. It was one of the nastiest shocks I ever had hearing the footsteps coming up the stairs. I could tell it wasn't you. I'm just thankful that I had the candlestick to defend myself with.'

'Is there any sign of life yet?'

'Well, he's breathing, but he hasn't opened his eyes, if that's what you mean. Funny, I would never have thought Mr Trigger was dangerous to women.'

Oyster poured the tea. 'What are we going to do if he doesn't recover? We can't have people coming into the house.' Even as she was speaking, she put down the teapot and glanced out of the kitchen window towards the end of the garden. She had the answer herself.

Juke Box Music

John Malcolm

Juke Box Music

THE GUESTS WERE STARTING TO leave, murmuring their final sympathies, and he approved of the way she stood near the door to bid them farewell without making her stance too obvious or ceremonial. Altogether there were still about a dozen or so to go, but she was careful not to hurry each parting obsecration urging her to look after herself or to depend on the speaker's support in the lonely days to come. She was composed and listened attentively, so that the offer was taken seriously, responded to with gravity. He knew, therefore, that there was still a little longer to look round the room and take in the work which Stan had preserved domestically for himself and for her benefit, work which, clearly, had special significance for him since the rest of his output would still be down at the gallery.

One of the things that struck him was that Stan, ironically, had been much interested in food. Not food in quantity, not in what might be called a good nosh, but in delicacies and tastes, in preparations and flavours. There was a tiny, icon-like gouache of a woman holding a plate of pomegranates. There was an oil of a flagged kitchen full of pots, with a couple preparing a delicate salad, involving fish. There was a pencil study of Junie herself, slicing lemons. It was not that Stan's painting concentrated exclusively on such things, by no means, although he had always been interested in domestic scenes. Down at the gallery there were all kinds of tableaux: landscapes with strange figures, Continental cafés and bars with life's remnants clinging to empty glasses, ennui in the manner of Sickert. There were, also, vivid street studies with jostling crowds, dances, circuses, railway stations and similar figurative realisms. But when he thought of Stan, the image his brain transmitted included, very often, little dishes of this and that, tasty morsels, an almost Gallic attitude to flora and fauna as gastronomic potential of some sort. Stan, he had to admit, had introduced him to many new culinary experiences without their necessarily having to be expensive. Stan was resourceful in that way; he would pick things on a country walk, cajole a single, gnarled root from a greengrocer, or emerge from a Covent Garden spice market with something extraordinary to put in a stew. It was no wonder that some of his paintings contained images of these unusual culinary interests, many of which had symbolic importance to the principal subject matter. Stan had been an intellectual, as well as an earthly painter.

The last guest slid through the passage door and out of the house so that, now, she turned to face him across the room. She was pale, the pallor emphasised by her black clothes, and her figure, small but abundant in the way that painters always seemed to like their women, looked diminished at this moment of heightened widowhood. He walked carefully round the table, with its remnants of food and wine, preparing to say his own farewell words, but she held up a hand.

'Just a moment, Dave,' she said, in a low tone. 'You can't go yet. Stan left something for you.'

'For me?' Surprise startled his valediction away. He stared at her, perplexed.

'Yes. It's upstairs. Will you come?'

'Of – of course.' Still mystified, he nodded. She moved without further words and led the way up the narrow stairs to the landing, turning then into what he knew was the spare bedroom of the little terraced house. He had, in the old days, slept there himself in the spare bed against which, he could see, a painting was propped with its face turned away from him. The painting had nonetheless been framed and, as she moved it from the bed, turning it to face him, she held it slightly tilted, so that the glass would not reflect the prancing images away, before she spoke to him.

'He wanted you to have it,' she said, looking at him expectantly, as though his reaction would be important. The chalky powder on her face had somehow coagulated into the creases, blown doubtless by the wind that had buffeted them all at the crematorium.

The painting stood between them, with her behind it. She was holding it like a shield with its bottom edge creasing the fabric of a stool she had now propped it on, to exhibit it, as though he were not familiar enough with it already.

133

'Oh,' he said, inadequately, swallowing a sudden surge of saliva, 'that's *Juke Box Music*.'

Her face moved slightly in what he took to be impatience at his lame response, perhaps even in irritation. She didn't say, 'Of course it's *Juke Box Music*, you ninny, don't be so wet, say something appropriate, try to rise to the occasion, speak up,' but she might have, from the quirk that twitched her cheek. She just held the frame of the painting and stared at him in pallid intensity so that he felt cornered, trapped, stuck into silence by all the adhesive knowledge that glued his mind into a defensive dumpling, an amorphous ball. He dared not speak at the unexpected sight of the thing. He thought that it had been sold, had gone far away, but here it was, back again, facing him with all the bravura colour and the extraordinary, distorted images for which Stan had been so famous, damn it, still was famous even if, now, he had been reduced to ashes so abruptly by the crematorium furnace.

'My God,' he said, suddenly finding the strength to unstick all that clogging emotion, the congealed defensive lump of reserve that warned him not to be too forthright. 'My God, I thought that they had sold that thing when, you know, when . . .'

He let his voice trail off. She had altered her expression. Knowledge was written all over it. Understanding deepened its lines. Her eyes rested on him now, not with their earlier intensity, heightened by the dark shadows around them, but with half-triumph, as though the sequence of events was following a pattern she had anticipated, had forecast, could control. She tilted the painting back a little more, as though to thrust its subject at him more prominently, to face him

134

with it so that he had to focus on it. Reluctantly, he stared at it.

The multicoloured juke box, flaring centrally in the darkened vertical rectangle, still vibrated colours like a striped and domed polychromatic sunset or an atomic explosion. Red, yellow and blue light radiated from it. Below its rounded, helmet-like upper structure spots of light beamed rays into the surrounding gloom. It was almost incandescent. Although the execution was slightly impressionistic it seemed vivid enough to think it possible to discern the mechanism that would have manipulated the records and played them. Although the painting was two-dimensional and silent, it seemed possible to feel that the juke box pulsated with light and sound, filling the space around it with the excitement of rhythmic booming and thudding as the flashing stripes from the brilliant bulbs caught the outlines of the figures hurtling round in confined space.

Stan had been very good at this sort of thing. In many ways this central source of heat, light and sound had been typical of Stan. Most of his paintings had a central focus, often towards the upper quarter of the design, that caught your attention and took it upwards, as a communicant kneeling before an altar rail might look upwards at the stained glass colours of a great pointed church window above him. It was a similar experience. When Stan had become famous the critics remarked on the semi-religious inspiration, the suppressed fervour behind the realistic figurative images of everyday people, often ugly people, caught in the attitudes that Stan painted. On the canvas in front of him now he saw, as he had not seen before, that due to a deliberate fault in perspective the dancing figures were below, no,

135

beneath the glowing juke box, under its aura so to speak, and that their ritual cavortings in the gloom penetrated by the juke box's shafts of light were like a frenzied ceremony enacted under a vast and intensely illuminated church window.

Ritual cavortings; he forced himself to look at the three figures in the foreground, the three figures that drew your attention from the juke box and contrasted with it so that there was a continuing shift between them and the bright light behind, so cleverly contraposed in the way for which Stan had become celebrated. In that sense his art was true to his life; Stan, he reflected bitterly, had combined within him those elements of the sacred and the profane which could be detected here in his work.

A man and two women pirouetted madly before him, the jive causing their limbs to be intertwined in an impossible indiarubber fling of positioning that the human frame could not possibly assume. The man, in the centre, had both drainpipe-trousered legs twirled out in different directions, so that the thick crepe soles of his spongy shoes were prominent in the air. His yellow tie snaked over his shoulder. One arm was round the woman on the left, who was thrown into a virtually horizontal position, twined round his waist in a rock-'n'roll slide that threw her legs out either side of the man's jacketed waist. The other arm held the woman on the right, a busty blonde with short skirt and high heels who turned half away, eyelids lowered, caught at the moment before the grasp on her arm would jerk her back into the powerful male figure's orbit. It was a crazy tableau, impossible, yet it conveyed vividly the whole essence of such dancing, painted by a man who must have understood it perfectly.

Stan had been a keen dancer.

He raised his eyes from the blonde on the right and looked at her, holding the painting up before him in knowing silence.

'Damn Stan,' he said. 'He caught you brilliantly there.'

She nodded slowly before she said what he had been dreading he would hear her say.

'And Vera,' she said. 'He caught Vera pretty well, too.'

He forced himself to look again at the woman on the left. She was dark, stockier than the blonde, thicker set. But of her fervour in the dance there was no doubt. Her face was alive with pleasure and concentration; her posture, almost horizontal and supported entirely by the man at waist level, was committed wholly, with entire confidence, to the physical fling of her gymnastic leap in obedience to the rhythm and to the bidding of the man. The wide cheekbones, the thick set of the mouth, the turn of the nose; that was Vera all right. There was no mistaking her.

He remembered the day he had called at the gallery unexpectedly, in response to a sudden impulse that diverted him from his usual route home from Berkeley Square towards Oxford Circus tube station. He'd turned away from the regular tread he normally made and had gone into Bond Street instead, wheeling right into the famous shopping thoroughfare and then left to reach Cork Street. He remembered thinking how it would surprise Vera, when he got home later, to tell her that he'd been back to see Stan's exhibition again, to see how the paintings looked when they were taken out of Stan's grubby studio in Wandsworth and put up properly in a Cork Street place. Vera regarded him as a man of habit, someone who you could depend on, not an artistic type at all, although he'd always liked Stan's work because they'd been at school together, came from the same shabby street, and he'd followed Stan's struggles to establish himself while he, Dave, got his articles and then good jobs as an accountant, working his way steadily while Stan had his ups and downs, mainly downs, so that he, Dave, had even had to lend Stan money from time to time, feeling as he did so the strength of his own tenacity and the insecurity behind Stan's artistic façade.

But then, eventually, Stan had come good and for the last year or so had started to make money, a lot of money. It had been exciting to know him recently, to see articles about him in the papers and his photograph in an arts review, to read his opinions and views about things. He stared at the central figure in the jive before him in the painting, the well-known face with its open, exultant mouth and its brows contracted in intense emotion, its eyes half-closed in sensual enjoyment. That was Stan, all right.

He never would forget the first time he'd seen that painting, in the gallery. It hadn't been amongst the pictures prepared for the exhibition in Stan's studio, the night he'd given Dave and Vera a private view before sending the lot off to Cork Street. Their excitement had been intense. Stan had opened a bottle of champagne and the four of them had celebrated, there at Stan's place amongst all the debris and paint, the canvases and frames that had cost so much, all ready to go. Months of work stood around them; Vera had peered excitedly at every single painting until Stan laughed at her, and then the two girls had taken their champagne, chattering, into the kitchen where some cold food had been prepared. The two men had stared at each other.

'Stan,' he'd said, he remembered it so well, 'I'm delighted for you. Absolutely over the moon.'

'Dave,' Stan had replied, clapping him on the shoulder, 'a lot of it is thanks to you. You always believed in me, Dave. You've supported me. I'll never forget that. I'll pay you back. I promise.'

He'll pay you back, he'd thought, later, after it happened. Pay you back.

The exhibition had been a great success. The reviews had all been excellent. Dave and Vera had attended the opening and seen it all. There was such a crush you could hardly get a look in at the pictures. People were too busy drinking wine and shouting to see them properly. That was why, a week or two later, he'd left his normal route and gone to look, just to show Vera that he wasn't the man of regular, dull routine that she thought and that he had taken the trouble to see his friend's paintings hung properly in his one-man show.

The gallery was getting ready to close down but the smooth girl who tended it had let him look round while he stared in wonder at the diversity of Stan's output. Then she took a painting out from behind the office corner where her desk had shielded it and started to write something down while he stared, his heart turning to a spike of painful ice, his legs going to matchwood under the weight of his thumping body.

The girl noticed him staring at it. 'Good, isn't it?' she said. 'It's a gouache, called *Juke Box Music*. It wasn't in the exhibition. We got one of those awkward customers – Japanese actually – who wanted a painting to buy and take away back to Japan immediately, but we're not allowing any of the exhibition paintings off the wall until it's over. Stan obliged by bringing this one in and letting the customer have it provided he paid a high price and it doesn't stay here and get mixed up with the exhibition work. I'm getting the documents together so it can go straight out tomorrow afternoon. The Jap is delighted, even though he really wanted that big one of the seaside.'

There was no doubt of who it was. There were Stan and his wife Junie, the blonde standing in front of him now, doing a painted rock'n'roll with Vera in a threesome that left no doubt of its significance. Stan could never resist that sort of thing. Religious his inspiration might be but secular was his attitude to relationships. The man in the painted dance was poised between two women, one of whom – Vera – had flung herself at him like a bobby-soxer and the other – Junie – was still held fast, ready to be jerked back when the movement of the dance dictated and the turns changed. Dave might be a steady, unimaginative accountant but of the movements in this fandango he was certain. Scraps of knowledge drifted into his darkened mind like shreds of debris fluttering down from a fatal airborne disaster. Remarks of Vera's. Attitudes of Stan's. Glances. Absences. Sudden passionate overtures and surrenders, like gifts bestowed by someone guilty. Tender understanding when he'd had to go to Manchester and Glasgow to audit some books, instead of the usual reproachful, guilt-inducing pique at his absence for a night or two. It had all added up, checked and balanced, like double-entry bookkeeping. The product of the addition was terrible.

He had marched abruptly out of the gallery, blindly, stamping down Cork Street without seeing anything or anyone until, stalking and turning, he found himself at Green Park station. Downstairs, in the hot tiled passages, was a row of telephones and, without thinking, he had launched himself at one of them, dialling Stan's number in cold fury, ready to scream hatred at him.

But the voice at the other end had been Junie's: calm, cool, detached.

'Hello?'

'Stan?' He was choked with rage.

'Dave?' Junie was surprised. 'Is that you?'

'Stan! Is Stan in? I want to speak to Stan!'

'No. No, he's away. Sketching in Devon. Are you all right? Is something wrong?'

'Wrong? Wrong?' He was shouting. 'I've just been to the gallery! And you ask me what's wrong?'

There was a silence.

'I've seen it! That painting!'

Junie's voice was low, controlled. 'What painting?'

'*Juke Box Music*! You tell him! Tell Stan! Tell him I've seen it!'

'Dave?'

'It'll only be there until tomorrow! Clever of him! But bad luck! I've seen it. Tell him I've seen it.'

Then he had slammed the phone down, shaking, and gone off to a pub. People did not seem to notice him as he downed a double whisky, then another. He was unremarkable. Looking at himself in the bar mirror he hated what he saw: an unremarkable man, an accountant of some sort, precise, methodical, neatly dressed. Nothing at all like Stan. And now Stan would make much more money than he ever would, and women like Vera would throw themselves at him not just for his bravura character and his dancing and food and artistic intelligence but for his money as well. It was no good him, Dave, screaming and shouting and thrashing Vera, it would achieve nothing. He was stifled by the uselessness of any action. Like the figures on the balance sheet of a defunct company, what was recorded was recorded, a chunk of past events and fated strivings graven on paper like the gouache under the glass he had stared at in the gallery. It had happened, it was done, it was irretrievable. The people in the pub began to notice him as he wept silently, his tears widening the wet circles on the false mahogany polish.

He said nothing to Vera. He regretted his outburst on the phone. He went about his business calmly, automatically, accepting an audit job up north as a means of avoiding everything there was to avoid. Stan's death, or rather the news of it, hit him like a hammer. Mushrooms! He had gone into hysterics in his hotel room. *Mushrooms.* A favourite gourmet enjoyment of Stan's. He and Stan and Junie had often gathered them together in the autumn, in woods and where land had been manured, Stan carefully instructing them on all the different types, cautioning them about the dangerous ones, teaching them how to look and where. Mushrooms: supposedly endowed with special properties. To be cooked in Stan's special way and eaten specially, intimately, yes, intimately. He thought of all the paintings and the food in them, paintings which now, over at the gallery, would fetch upwards of half a million pounds, perhaps even more. Nothing increased art values like the premature death of a talented performer. It would need careful management.

'I – I don't understand,' he stammered at Junie, who was still observing him gravely, her black clothes now looking creased and tired, as though they had done their job and were anxious to be folded and pressed and put away neatly for another occasion a long time off.

'The Japanese never got it,' she said. 'I went to the gallery and took it away. After your call.'

'But – but why me? Why did Stan want me to have it?'

Her face remained unemotional. 'He had some time to think about it. At the hospital, while they were trying to save him. I'm afraid it was very painful. Those natural poisons always are.' She moved a little closer, letting the painting tilt back again, and took his hand sympathetically in her own warm, dry one.

'How did Vera's funeral go?' she asked.

The Trouble with Trains

Mike Ripley

The Trouble with Trains

'I HAVE ALWAYS BEEN LUCKY with trains,' said the dapper little Belgian.

'They're useful,' said the Inspector, 'for getting up to the opera, or establishing alibis.'

'Try not to use them, meself,' said the Aristocrat, adjusting his monocle.

The Inspector looked at the Aristocrat and wearily curled a lip. 'Do you know how close that came to a Bertie Wooster?'

'Yes, I do,' nodded the Aristocrat. 'It's a thin red line we tread in this game, isn't it?'

But that's the trouble with trains. They encourage you to play games because while you are on them you are cut off from reality; caught in a funnel of time and space beyond your control. And if the train is stopped – stuck in an unseasonally heavy snowfall in the deserted Lincolnshire countryside – and you're only on it in the first place because you are playing a game . . .

'How did we get into this?' the Inspector asked, but he was staring out of the window, the squares of the carriages' lights reflected in the piled snowdrifts alongside the track.

'You know that very well, old boy,' said the Belgian. 'We have to keep the writers happy, as well as the fans.'

'Watch it, your accent's slipping,' snarled the Inspector.

'Well just be thankful you do not 'ave to talk like zis.'

The Inspector nodded. 'Yes, I suppose that's something.'

'Oh come on, you two,' said the Aristocrat. 'The conference was fun and we didn't have to sit through all three days. We had some decent meals – and breakfast in the hotel wasn't half bad. I put away enough this morning to feed half the Royal Shakespeare Company in a lean patch. Look on it as a free holiday.'

'In Leeds?' challenged the Inspector.

'Well, yes, there was that. But they've laid on this special train and you don't often get to travel in authentic 1930s Pullmans these days, do you? And at least we have some privacy and the champagne keeps arriving every time we press that little buzzer thing . . .'

'And even British Rail should be able to chill it properly, with all this snow and ice about,' observed the Belgian.

'But what about *them*?'

'Oh, I suppose we'll have to go and mingle with Second Class sooner or later,' conceded the Aristocrat, 'and sing for our supper. It's the crime writers who keep us going, you know.'

'True,' said the Belgian, 'though *en masse* they can be quite daunting.'

Trapped on a British Rail special train in an unseasonally heavy snowfall. One Pullman car of sanity where the guests of honour dined and rested in private before rejoining the two hundred crime writers busily stripping the buffet bar at the other end of the train. Keeping their spirits up until the track was cleared, all of them delighted that the delay would give them longer to rub shoulders with the embodiment of their imaginations. Some of them posted as guards along the train to catch the first glimpse of their heroes, who sat in their reserved compartment. A locked room within a much longer, brightly lit, immobile, locked tube.

'Was everything satisfactory, gentlemen?' asked the white-coated steward from the compartment doorway.

'Simply splendid,' said the Aristocrat.

'We don't get many chances to push the boat out on the catering side,' said the steward chattily. 'That's why we like these special trains. The Royals have travelled in this carriage, you know. That was a trip, I can tell you.'

'Perhaps zat one was – how you say – on time?' the little Belgian asked softly.

'Well, no, actually . . . Can I get you anything else, gentlemen? We may be here for some time. May I be so bold as to suggest a *tisane*, a bottle of Tokay and a pint of bitter?' He grinned inanely.

'Three brandies – big jobs,' said the Inspector curtly.

'Certainly, sir'. The steward took his leave.

'I suppose we could do a question-and-answer session to entertain our hosts,' said the Aristocrat thoughtfully.

'Again?' sighed the Belgian.

'How about bloody charades?'

'Don't be so depressed, old boy.'

'I thought I was supposed to be.'

'Well, we'll have to do something for them. Only manners, after all.'

The dapper Belgian stabbed at his last piece of cheese with a knife. 'I think this cheese came with the Pullman car,' he said to himself. Then, to his fellows: 'How about getting them to exercise . . .'

'If he says "little grey cells" I'll hit him,' the Inspector whispered.

' . . . their imaginations. Let us give them a scenario for a murder. And let us begin with a train stranded in an unseasonally heavy snowfall.'

And that was when the shot rang out.

Of course, it might have sounded like a shot, though many would have described it as a muffled pop. That's the trouble with trains: they distort things. But there was no doubt about the scream or the noise of a compartment door slamming open which followed.

The three heroes stared at each other.

'It's a set-up,' said the Inspector.

'One of their stupid games, no doubt,' said the Aristocrat.

'But did you not just say,' the Belgian said cuttingly, 'that it was only good manners to join in their games?'

The Aristocrat flipped his eyes up to the ancient light fittings and the net luggage racks. 'I suppose we have to go through with it, however embarrassing. Come on, then.'

The Belgian slid open the compartment door and

poked his balding, not-quite-egg-shaped head out into the corridor. He turned back to his companions and shrugged.

As the Inspector and the Aristocrat joined him, the steward appeared to their right bearing a tray of drinks.

'Sorry for the delay, gents. Had to take an order to the kitchen for Compartment B.'

The heroes looked at each other knowingly. The Belgian held up the forefinger of his right hand, indicating for the steward to wait. He wished he had remembered the pearl- grey gloves.

The Aristocrat raised a finger also and pointed to the second compartment to their left, the door of which lay open.

'Let's get on with it,' said the Inspector, squeezing between his colleagues.

There was a table laid out for dinner in Compartment B exactly as their own had been, but dinner had yet to be served. Apart from two glasses, an open bottle of champagne in an ice bucket and the cutlery, there was nothing on the table except the slumped form of a well-dressed middle-aged man.

'*Voilà*,' said the Belgian.

'The body,' said the Inspector.

'I wonder how long we've got?' said the Aristocrat.

'Bloody hell,' said the steward.

The Inspector stepped into the compartment.

'Touch nothing!' snapped the small Belgian.

'Oh, give us a break.'

'What's going on?' whispered the steward.

'Did you pass anyone in the corridor when you brought the drinks?' asked the Aristocrat casually, helping himself to one of the brandy glasses.

'No, not a soul. Is he dead?' The steward stretched his neck to see over the Belgian's shoulder, the remaining brandies dipping dangerously.

'And what is back there?'

'Just the old-fashioned guard's van, then the real guard's van and mail coach.'

'Then unless our criminal is a member of British Rail staff, our case is almost solved,' agreed the Belgian.

The Inspector put a hand to the slumped man's neck, then recoiled. He turned to his fellow travellers, his face white and his eyes wide.

'What's the matter, old boy? Don't agree?' The Aristocrat sipped his brandy. 'Want to spin it out a bit? Establish motive and all that? No-one went by our compartment, so they must have gone to the rear of . . .'

'No . . . no . . .' The Inspector rubbed his hand down his jacket. The hand that had touched the body. 'He really is dead. It's a real stiff.'

'*Mon Dieu*,' breathed the Belgian, forgetting himself for a moment.

'Nice try, old boy. Well, we'll go along with it, won't we? Play the game and all that?'

'Hang on.' The little Belgian stooped over the corpse. 'He's right. This guy's not breathing and look – there's blood!'

'Hell's teeth.'

'Quick, pull the communication cord,' said the steward.

'We're not moving, you idiot.' The Inspector relieved him of another glass and downed the contents. 'Go and find the guard, or the Fat Controller, or whoever can take charge. Move it!'

The steward scurried off to the rear of the train.

The three heroes stood and stared at the body, then at each other.

'No-one could have laid this on,' said the Inspector.

'It would be fun to try and solve it before the guard comes,' said the Aristocrat.

'Then let us try,' said the Belgian. 'Why not?'

The Inspector turned and gently hit his forehead on the edge of the compartment door. 'Are you out of your mind? Who do you think we are?'

'My point – *précisément!*'

Does the train leave the platform or the platform leave the train? Isolated and self-contained, reality can blur in trains. That's the trouble with them.

'But even if this were real – the body is, I know – but if we really were who we are . . .'

'The victim was called Cooper,' said the Aristocrat languidly.

The others followed the line of his eyes to the luggage rack and the expensive suitcase complete with matching leather address fob.

'Mr A.D. Cooper, of Redhill in Surrey,' the Aristocrat read.

'Then who was the woman? Do we *cherchez la femme*? It is traditional.'

'Woman?'

'*Bien sûr*. This is a smoking compartment and look, in the ashtray – a filter tip with lipstick.'

'Not to mention her coat on the other rack,' said the Inspector reluctantly. 'What about the wound?'

The three heroes formed a semi-circle around the man slumped over the table and in unison, bent their knees until three pairs of heroic eyes were level with the head.

'It's difficult to see without moving the head,' said the Aristocrat.

'We must touch nothing,' said the Belgian.

'It looks like he's been shot between the eyes,' said the Inspector. 'There's a round mark, like a coin. And . . . blood.'

'But not much,' said the Belgian.

'How much should there be?' asked the Aristocrat. 'That was a serious question. I've never actually seen . . .'

'Neither have I,' said the other two as they stood up.

Somewhere down the train a door slammed.

'So what do the little . . . *Pardon*. What can we deduce? He was a rich man?'

'Comfortable enough to hire this compartment and lay on a dinner for the missing lady,' said the Aristocrat. 'What's our betting? Stockbroker?'

'Advertising man, judging by the suit,' said the Inspector.

'Was it his wife, or a bit on the side?'

'Someone he knew very well,' said the Belgian. 'We heard no raised voices, there is no sign of a struggle. He was not expecting to be attacked.'

'Looks more like a celebration, with the champagne,' the Inspector observed. 'But the glasses are clean so they never got that far.'

'Perhaps they argued over the menu,' suggested the Aristocrat facetiously.

'The British Rail do not provide sufficient choice for an argument,' said the Belgian dismissively. 'Yet if this was planned, how could the woman – wife or mistress –

154

know that the train would stop here? This was not planned.'

'So it was an impulse killing.'

'A crime of passion? The end of an affair, perhaps?'

'You mean he told her he was dumping her so she whipped out a gun and shot him?'

'*Un petit* . . . conventional. We should expect the unexpected.'

'You mean she dumped him, so he shot himself out of remorse?'

'Stranger things have happened, old boy.'

'In fiction, maybe.'

'Then where's the bloody gun?'

'Removed by some devilishly ingenious automatic device, no doubt. Or carried by the woman's real husband, who shoots his rival, grabs the fair lady and leaps off the train into a snow drift, leaving two sets of prints in the snow . . .'

'*Mais* – that is what she wants us to think, for this woman is very clever. Very clever indeed.'

'You mean . . . there was no second man?'

'What about a second woman?'

'What about *no woman at all*? After all, there is no handbag here. A woman is likely to leave a coat but not a handbag, or is that what we were supposed to think? Could a man get away with wearing a fur coat such as the one on the luggage rack?'

'What if . . . ?'

'Excuse me, gentlemen,' said a new voice from the doorway.

They turned to see a young man in a railway issue anorak.

'I'm Blunt.'

'I'll bet,' said the Inspector.

'Of British Rail Transport Police. We sometimes get gatecrashers on these special trains, or perhaps over-keen train spotters.'

'So you disguise yourself as one,' breathed the Aristocrat.

Blunt stepped into the compartment and surveyed the scene. 'Ah yes, I see it now.'

The three heroes looked at each other and then at Blunt.

'How it happened. Poor Mr Cooper there, how tragic. Of course he always knew he suffered from a rare bone disease which meant he had a particularly thin skull, unlike most people. But who would have thought that the champagne cork going off like that and hitting him between the eyes would have killed him? A million-to-one blow. Quite fantastic.' Blunt sighed briefly. 'All in a day's work to you chaps, though, I suppose. I hope that's not as heartless as it sounds.'

The three heroes examined their shoes, or in one case, his spats.

'You must have noticed that the champagne was open and the front of Mr Cooper's shirt was soaked with the stuff. I expect you'd worked it all out, eh? What a pity it should happen on their wedding anniversary. Ah, there's the weapon.'

Blunt crouched and put a hand under the table. He emerged with a champagne cork still surrounded by its metal foil and wire cage.

'I think one of you may have kicked it there,' said Blunt.

'How . . .?' started three voices.

'Mrs Cooper ran straight to the guard's van and told

156

us all about it. Quite distraught she was, and I found her story a bit much at first, I can tell you. Still, it was so crazy it must be true. She'd hardly make it up, would she? Not with you three in the next compartment!'

And when even fantasy begins to blur, what then? It is a constant trouble with trains.

'We'll be moving again in a minute, the line's clear and we've radioed ahead so we can pick up a doctor in Grantham and the police will meet us in London. I would appreciate it if you would help calm the passengers until we get there. I know it will take quite a performance, all those crime writers wanting to know how you found a real live body. Well, you know what I mean. And no doubt the press will be waiting for us in London.'

The three heroes looked at each other.

'Did you say you could radio ahead?' asked the Inspector.

'Yes,' said Blunt, wondering why three pairs of eyes had twinkled and three slow smiles appeared.

'Can I call my agent?' they said together.

Back in reality the only real trouble with trains emerges. They shake up good champagne cruelly.

Widow's Might

Margaret Yorke

Widow's Might

MRS WATSON WATCHED AS THE gardener, high on a ladder, lopped the branches of the tall palm in the hotel garden. Heavy trusses of berries fell to the ground, and the trunk of the tree bore smooth white spherical scars where he made his cuts. So death came, chopping down those who had lived too long or who had flirted with danger, or were doomed.

She sat in a comfortable chair in the shade of a pomegranate, a book on her knee. A gentle breeze stirred the leaves of the red hibiscus and the blue flowers of a plumbago which sprawled on a trellis beside the steps leading to the terrace. Though it was November, the island, warmed by the Gulf Stream, was never cold and seldom uncomfortably hot. Its jagged coastline bore a rash of large hotels, but Mrs Watson's, one of the oldest, was also the most expensive and the most luxurious. Here, the ratio of staff to clients was almost one to one and, lapped in care, the pampered guests felt worries, aches and pains slip away, forgotten.

Mrs Watson and her husband had first visited the island when on a cruise. Their liner had steamed in at daybreak and they had spent an interesting day, visiting the cathedral and driving into the country in a taxi. They had passed banana plantations, waterfalls, and reached mountain areas where the air was fresh, and they had had tea at this hotel where now she sat alone. Her husband had approved it as a suitable place for them to visit in the future: only there had been no future for Mr Watson for that very night, en route to Gibraltar, he had had a heart attack in their cabin on 'A' deck and had died within minutes. Mrs Watson and the coffin had flown home to a well-attended funeral at the local crematorium where representatives of the many organisations with which the deceased had been connected, diluted with members of his staff and several workmen from the current sites he was developing, made up the congregation. There were no children of their union, no son to lead her to her pew, and Mrs Watson proudly walked alone.

Mr Watson had been a property developer, and by the terms of his will, so long as the business prospered, she was well provided for: however, now it was in the hands of his partner. They had amalgamated when both were competing for a particularly desirable site in the centre of a new town: a Dutch auction over it had seemed pointless at the time, and, since then, the two had worked well together. Now the partner was obliged to pay Mrs Watson a large portion annually of his profits. This was satisfactory for several years, until the partner spread himself too far, the banks called in their loans, and the business fell apart.

Mrs Watson was only forty-five years old when she became a widow. She was still trim and shapely, her hair burnished gold, rinsed regularly by Sandra at Bandbox Coiffures, and her complexion smooth. She found life hard alone, for Mr Watson, fifteen years older than she, had cherished her all the twenty-five years of their life together. She had worked in his office as a bookkeeper: she was good at figures, and very pretty, and had soon attracted the attention of the rising Mr Watson, who was looking about for a suitable wife, something he had been too busy to do sooner, for what was the point of amassing a fortune if you had no-one to spend it on?

Mrs Watson, then Madge Fraser, had grown up in a semi-detached villa in Luton, where her father was a bank clerk and her mother devotedly kept house, running up frocks for Madge on her Singer machine and cooking nourishing meals, in between keeping the house spotless. In those days women were not expected to strive on all fronts as mothers, wives and wage-earners, and couples who found themselves incompatible or bored with one another usually stayed together in conditions of civilised truce until or unless one of them was tempted away by a new love. However, Madge's parents were fond of each other and of their only child, pinning their ambitions and hopes on her, and when she married her boss, just as happened in the magazines her mother read, their joy and pride were boundless.

Madge went to live in Bletchley, in a new four-bedroomed house with two bathrooms, a study and a utility room as well as a large lounge and dining-room. It stood in nearly an acre of garden, all laid out and planted by a nursery-man. Like her mother, Madge cleaned and baked, and in her spare time did *gros point* as there was no daughter to sew for or take to dancing-class, nor was there an economical reason to dressmake for herself. She went to flower-arranging classes and art lessons to fill up her time, and gradually she became a gardener, rearranging what the nursery-man had planned and devising new corners and grottoes. She joined a gardening club and went with them on excursions to stately homes where she secretly broke off shoots of plants to propagate through cuttings, building up a remarkable collection of shrubs unique in their neighbourhood. Mr Watson was proud of her green fingers and had no notion as to the true source of her acquisitions.

After Madge's father died, her mother stayed on in the house in Luton, but she accompanied the Watsons on their holidays, staying in hotels in Spain and villas in Greece, which she found rather hot. Eventually she expired peacefully in her sleep after a bout of flu, giving in death no more trouble than she had given in life and leaving Madge her worldly possessions, the house now free of its mortgage and her few pieces of jewellery.

Madge sold up and used the money to open a florist's shop which she named Rosa's, where she installed as assistant a woman she met in her flower-arranging class. Mr Watson was amused at the venture and pleased with its success. 'Madge's toy,' he called it, 'her baby, seeing as we've none of our own.' The enterprise flourished and she opened a second shop in another district, then a third. Her foraging trips to alien gardens grew fewer as the business absorbed her surplus energy and her administrative skills. By the time of Mr Watson's demise she was prospering in her own right, so that when his partner went officially bankrupt – though in fact he had siphoned away considerable funds in the name of his wife and daughter, enough to enable him to start up again when his debts were written off – she was able to maintain her customary standard of living. She continued to reside at Greenways, which property alone was now worth a considerable sum, enough to fund a comfortable life for Madge if her florist shops failed. But they did not: they expanded and throve as Madge took on able managers to whom she paid bonuses on turnover.

But she did not enjoy being a widow.

It was not simply that she missed the comfort of Mr Watson's protection, his big warm body, his interest and his pampering: it was the rest of the condition that irked. She was unpartnered now, half of what had been a whole, an outcast in paired society. When travelling, her single state seemed as if it was a crime. People shunned her. Except in the best hotels, she was given an inferior room and at far higher cost than the rate for one half of a couple. Her table in the dining-room would be near a service door or in a draught, and the wine waiter would ignore her, although she always ordered a half bottle of the best local wine available. Sometimes she would be served rapidly, course following upon course so that she could be removed swiftly from the scene; at other times she would be neglected. Mrs Watson never returned to hotels which treated her in this manner, but here nothing was too much trouble: she was tended ceremoniously.

Here, it was the guests to whom she seemed invisible, and Mrs Watson knew the reason: it was fear. The women were warned of the isolation that would be theirs when they became widows themselves, as statistically was quite probable, and the men were reminded of their own mortality.

When she was younger, Mrs Watson had posed a different threat, though at the time she had been unaware of it because it had never occurred to her to embark on any sort of affair; with hindsight, now, she recognised that she had been still pretty, even desirable, when she began to travel alone. At home she had been pursued, to her naive surprise, by one of her husband's cronies, an untimely widower, but she had soon made her lack of interest plain. She needed no meal ticket for her security, and her energies were directed towards her own business and her garden, where an aged man helped her to keep down the weeds and cut the grass.

She observed the couples who came and went during her visits to various luxurious hotels, and she wondered which would still be together the following year, which parted either by death or by divorce. Because the hotels were expensive, most of the couples she encountered were older guests whose families had grown and flown, but sometimes there were honeymooners, shyly young among their elders and benignly smiled upon, and there were other couples, obviously paired without the formality of a marriage certificate.

Mrs Watson watched an elderly man and his wife cross the lawn and stiffly mount the stairs that led from the garden to the wide verandah where teas were served. The man carried his wife's knitting in its floral bag: Mrs Watson had observed her turning the heel of a warm olive green sock; her own mother had knitted socks like that when Mrs Watson was herself a school-girl, during the war. Her father, myopic and flat-footed, had been spared the call-up but he was an Air Raid Warden and her mother was a member of a knitting-party. Mrs Watson had not realised that people still wore hand-knitted socks. She wondered what work, if any, the husband had done – he was long past retiring age. With them were their son – unmistakeable because so like the mother – and a daughter-in-law, a pale, elegant woman who had about her an air of confident distinct-ion. Breeding, thought Mrs Watson, breaking off a spur of the red hibiscus which, if it took, would replace one she had lost in a recent severe winter; breeding gave you that air of quiet arrogance, but would it be of help if your husband was struck down prematurely and you were left alone? Who, then, would open doors for you, carry hand luggage, park the car after dropping you at the door of wherever you were going, complain if a room was unsuitable or the service bad? She would not be left penniless, that elegant woman; there would be insur-ance if not family wealth, but that was not the only provision she would require.

The younger couple passed Mrs Watson's chair, and the woman saw Mrs Watson drop her hibiscus sprig into her bag.

At dinner, Mrs Watson sat not far from the quartet. Ready to be pleasant, she smiled across at them but was ignored as she consumed her lobster bisque, her gnocchi, her chicken, then her chocolate mousse.

Leaving the dining-room while the four were still eating, passing behind the younger woman's chair, Mrs Watson heard her speak.

'That woman was stealing sprigs from the plants,' she said in a thin, clear voice. 'I saw her do it. An hibiscus shoot today. What will it be tomorrow? A pomegranate, do you suppose? Perhaps she could grow one from the fruit.'

'Charlotte, don't! She'll hear,' shushed the mother, whose own voice was more penetrating than her daughter-in-law's.

'Who cares?' was the answer. 'It should be reported. If every guest did it, there would be nothing left. She's like those people who come to Ferbingham. They've stripped whole sprays from the mulberry, and some of the choicest shrubs are decimated. We've had to put notices up and we may have to employ special patrols.'

Mrs Watson, moving slowly, had heard most of this. So they lived at Ferbingham, did they? She had visited that garden and she had a shoot from the well-known mulberry rooted and beginning to sprout. Ferbingham was a Tudor mansion opened on certain selected dates in the year; Mrs Watson knew that the elder couple had moved to the dower house some years ago, leaving their son to manage the estate.

She made up her mind that night. The supercilious Charlotte should be this year's victim. Every time she went away she chose one, and had been foiled only once when her target had left before she could carry out her plan, leaving no time for a substitute to be picked. Mrs Watson never returned for a second visit to any hotel, however enjoyable her stay; it did not do to retrace one's steps lest a second incident might seem more than coincidence.

Last year, in Montreux, vulgarity had been the trigger. She had felt shame, witnessing the brash conduct of a couple who, as they acquired money and the spurious status it bought, had not acquired manners to match. This year it was an excess of conceit and condescension that were significant.

Last year, near a cable car station, there had been a fatal fall from a cliff. No-one had suspected the white-haired widow – Madge had abandoned her gold rinse years ago – who reported witnessing the fall of being its cause. The man had strayed away from his wife: the side of the mountain was steep and the sudden shove totally unexpected.

This year opportunity and method might be less easy.

Mrs Watson stalked her prey and heard them order a taxi to visit the Botanical Gardens which, she knew, were high on a hillside; she had been there already, herself.

Mrs Watson was there an hour before they arrived. She had walked round seeking possible hazards and admired lilies and orchids, glossy scarlet anthurium which looked waxen, strelitzia – the birds of paradise flowers – the pendulous trumpets of datura, which was a poisonous plant. She leaned on the walking stick she often carried – a versatile accessory – and gazed across the ravine dividing the hills to where the distant sea shone blue. There was no cruise ship in today and, late in the season as it was, there were few visitors to the gardens that day. Then she saw the elderly mother approaching along a side path, pausing to gaze at various plants; she was with her son. Looking about, Mrs Watson saw no sign of Charlotte or her father-in-law. Perhaps they had decided not to come?

It proved to be so. She watched carefully, making sure they were absent: so much the better for her purpose. The old woman and her son – his name was Hugo, Mrs Watson had heard it spoken – consulted the labels attached to various plants, moving slowly to a viewpoint where, protected by a low stone parapet built less than a yard from the sheer drop beyond, one could gaze in safety at the vista. She made an entry in a small red notebook where she had listed plants seen and identified. As she wrote down the name of an unusual cactus – she did not like cacti – fate played into her hands, for Hugo, ahead of his mother and approaching the spot where Mrs Watson was waiting, called out to the old lady.

'There'll be a wonderful view here,' he told her.

'You go ahead,' she replied. 'You know I don't care for heights. I'll wait for you near those lilies we liked. We might note some varieties and see if we can order the bulbs.'

She turned and walked down a cobbled path, vanishing from sight round a bend, and Hugo advanced towards where Mrs Watson stood. She surreptitiously dropped her notebook over the parapet and, before uttering small cries of distress, leaned over to poke at it with her stick till it lodged in a small bush on the edge of the ravine.

Hugo, ever civil, although aware that this was the woman his wife had seen snipping cuttings from plants in the hotel garden, made concerned inquiries as to what was wrong.

'My references,' cried Mrs Watson. 'My check list of names – flowers I've seen and identified, to report to my local flower club. I've dropped it. So silly of me,' and she leaned over the parapet gazing at the spot where, only just out of reach, the small notebook reposed.

'It's important, is it?' asked Hugo.

'Vital. It's the only record I've got,' Mrs Watson declared. 'I have to give a talk to the group when I get home.' She looked at him. 'You're very tall. Couldn't you reach it?'

'Hardly,' said Hugo, with a grimace. 'I might simply knock it over the hillside down the ravine.'

'I'll climb over and get it,' said Mrs Watson. 'Perhaps you'd just hold my arm while I do so, to steady me?'

'I can't let you do that,' exclaimed Hugo, looking aghast at Mrs Watson, five foot two inches tall and no longer young. 'I'll have a go. My arms are longer.'

'Oh no!' Hand to mouth, Mrs Watson demurred.

Hugo, carried back to boyhood days of derring-do, swung one leg over the low wall, then the other, crouching, now out of sight of anyone who might come towards them. The ledge was narrow, but though he held the wall at first, he found he could not reach the notebook without releasing his grasp. He had just seized it when he felt a sudden jab in the small of his back. Mrs Watson, pushing with all her might, had feared she would lack the strength to make him lose his balance, but she succeeded, and uttering only a strangled cry, he tore at a bush which broke off in his hand as he hurtled towards the valley.

Mrs Watson held back her piteous cries and shrieks for a few vital seconds, making sure he had fallen satisfactorily and fatally far before rasing the alarm. When retrieved, Hugo's body bore a great many bruises, and the sharp round one caused by the ferrule of her walking stick aroused no special interest. She said, with truth, that he had insisted on climbing over the wall to rescue her notebook which most foolishly she had dropped.

171

'I tried to persuade him it was of no consequence,' she declared, weeping gently. 'But he insisted.'

The notebook was still clutched in his hand. It contained, as she had said, a list of a great many plants but it was not just what she had seen on the island; it was of more significance, for each plant noted was special. The oleander was a memory of Crete, and an accident in a swimming-pool; an agapanthus meant a fall at Lindos. A gentian reminded her of Lausanne and sleeping pills in brandy, followed by a lakeside walk in the dusk. There were others.

The cactus should represent Hugo.

It didn't do to mock at widows. Their ranks increased all the time. Now it was Charlotte's turn.

Who would be next?

Biographical Notes on the Contributors

Biographical Notes on the Contributors

Robert Barnard has spent most of his adulthood behind a desk, either marking student essays or writing detective novels, but since he has mostly done this abroad (first in Australia, then in Norway) people often comment on his adventurous life. He has now moved back to the UK, lives in Leeds, and still spends much of his life behind a desk.

Simon Brett is the author of over forty books, of which more than half are crime novels. He is the creator of the amateur detectives Charles Paris and Mrs Pargeter, and wrote the radio and television series *After Henry*. He has edited numerous anthologies and is the presenter of Radio Four's *Dear Diary*. A former department-store Father Christmas, he is also a former radio producer, a former television producer and a former Chairman of the Crime Writers' Association.

Michael Gilbert Seven years a schoolmaster, seven years a soldier, thirty-four years a solicitor: and all the time a writer, from the earliest years when he was writing one-act plays for the boys (one in which Medina Sidonia was seasick, thus accounting for the defeat of the Spanish Armada, is still remembered). Since then thirty books, four stage plays, a lot of television and radio and umpteen short stories. Also a long-suffering wife, seven children and eleven grandchildren. *Quantum sufficit* as the doctors say.

H.R.F. Keating met one day in 1964 a man just back from a job in advertising in Bombay, and, on the strength of his enthusiasm about a vague notion of writing a detective story set in India, embarked on a book called *The Perfect Murder* with as its hero a Bombay CIDwalla, Inspector Ghote. The book won the Gold Dagger award, Ghote went on to feature in sixteen other novels and several dozen short stories and Harry Keating found himself inextricably entangled with India evermore.

Roger Longrigg was born in Edinburgh in 1929, brought up in Scotland, Iraq, Palestine and New England and educated at Bryanston and Magdalen College, Oxford. After doing military service in the Middle East, he worked in various advertising agencies until 1968 since when he has been a full-time writer. He is the author of over fifty books under eight different names. He has also published numerous short stories and articles and has written for the theatre, films, television and radio. Mr Longrigg now lives in rural Hampshire with his wife and three daughters.

Peter Lovesey At fourteen, Peter Lovesey mugged up the history of his birthplace, Whitton, Middlesex, and won a competition to celebrate the 1951 Festival of Britain. After Hampton School, Reading University and the RAF, he taught in further education. A keen athletics 'nut', he started writing about the history of running. By switching to running as fiction, he won a second competition with his first crime novel, *Wobble to Death*. He is the author of eighteen novels and many short stories and his work has appeared on radio, television and film. He is Chairman of the Crime Writers' Association.

John Malcolm has written eight crime novels since 1984. His books feature Tim Simpson, an art investment specialist with a London merchant bank, whose acquisitions involve him in the desperate dealings and violence of the art and antiques underworld in Europe and North America. Since John Malcolm is also the author of two standard reference works on antique furniture which have been in print since 1968, and his wife, until recently, was a picture restorer, he has used his extensive knowledge in his fiction. He is also the author of several short stories published in the UK and the USA and continues to write articles and books on art and antiques. His experience as an international businessman has been invaluable in the background for his fiction, which is set not only in England but in Europe and North and South America. He was born in

Manchester and spent part of his boyhood in Uruguay before returning to school and university in England. He and his wife live in Sussex from whence they travel extensively.

Mike Ripley's first comedy crime novel, *Just Another Angel*, appeared in 1988. Since then he has written three more, numerous short stories and pieces of non-fiction on crime writing and has become the crime critic of the *Daily Telegraph*. He is a founder member of the 'Fresh Blood' group of younger, more streetwise British crime writers. He has yet to give up the day job in the brewing industry, where he writes and broadcasts about British beer and pubs.

Margaret Yorke was a driver in the WRNS for the last three years of the war. She was the first woman ever to work in Christ Church Library, Oxford, where she made the card catalogue. She enjoys the theatre, reading, music, gardening and travel. Research for her books constantly provides new interests such as the need for penal reform and revision of the judicial system. For thirty-five years she has lived in Buckinghamshire where she has seen many sociological and environmental changes. She is a past Chairman of the Crime Writers' Association.

Scribners